FIRE ON THE MOUNTAIN

Anita Desai was born and educated in India. Her published works include adult novels, children's books and short stories. *Clear Light of Day* (1980), *In Custody* (1984) and *Fasting, Feasting* (1999) were all shortlisted for the Booker Prize, and *The Village by the Sea* won the *Guardian* Award for Children's Fiction in 1982. Anita Desai is a Fellow of the Royal Society of Literature in London, of the American Academy of Arts and Letters in New York and of Girton College at the University of Cambridge. She teaches in the Writing Program at M.I.T. and divides her time between India, Boston, Massachusetts and Cambridge, England. *In Custody* was recently filmed by Merchant Ivory Productions.

ALSO BY ANITA DESAI

Anita Desai

FIRE ON THE MOUNTAIN

VINTAGE

Published by Vintage 1999

8 10 9 7

First published in Great Britain by
William Heinemann Ltd 1977

Vintage
Random House, 20 Vauxhall Bridge Road,
London SW1V 2SA

Random House Australia (Pty) Limited
20 Alfred Street, Milsons Point, Sydney
New South Wales 2061, Australia

Random House New Zealand Limited
18 Poland Road, Glenfield, Auckland 10, New Zealand

Random House (Pty) Limited
Endulini, 5a Jubilee Road, Parktown 2193, South Africa

The Random House Group Limited Reg. No. 954009

www.randomhouse.co.uk

A CIP catalogue record for this book
is available from the British Library

ISBN 0 0994 2848 2

Papers used by Random House are natural, recyclable products
made from wood grown in sustainable forests. The manufacturing
processes conform to the environmental regulations of the country
of origin

Printed and bound in Great Britain by
Cox & Wyman Ltd, Reading, Berkshire

For Ruth and Jhab

Quotations from *The Pillow Book of Sei Shonagon*
translated by Ivan Morris 1967 by permission of
the Oxford University Press.

Frontispiece from a drawing by C. S. H. Jhabvala

Contents

PART I

Nanda Kaul at Carignano

Chapter 1

Nanda Kaul paused under the pine trees to take in their scented sibilance and listen to the cicadas fiddling invisibly under the mesh of pine needles when she saw the postman slowly winding his way along the Upper Mall. She had not gone out to watch for him, did not want him to stop at Carignano, had no wish for letters. The sight of him, inexorably closing in with his swollen bag, rolled a fat ball of irritation into the cool cave of her day, blocking it stupidly: bags and letters, messages and demands, requests, promises and queries, she had wanted to be done with them all, at Carignano. She asked to be left to the pines and cicadas alone. She hoped he would not stop.

Everything she wanted was here, at Carignano, in Kasauli. Here, on the ridge of the mountain, in this quiet house. It was the place, and the time of life, that she had wanted and prepared for all her life – as she realized on her first day at Carignano, with a great, cool flowering of relief – and at last she had it. She wanted no one and nothing else. Whatever else came, or happened here, would be an unwelcome intrusion and distraction.

This she tried to convey to the plodding postman with a cold and piercing stare from the height of the ridge onto his honest bull back. Unfortunately he did not look up at her on the hill-top but stared stolidly down at the dust piling onto his shoes as he plodded on. A bullock man, an oafish ox, she thought bitterly, and averted her eyes. She stepped backwards into the garden and the wind suddenly billowed up and threw the pine branches about as though to curtain her.

3

She was grey, tall and thin and her silk sari made a sweeping, shivering sound and she fancied she could merge with the pine trees and be mistaken for one. To be a tree, no more and no less, was all she was prepared to undertake.

What pleased and satisfied her so, here at Carignano, was its barrenness. This was the chief virtue of all Kasauli of course – its starkness. It had rocks, it had pines. It had light and air. In every direction there was a sweeping view – to the north, of the mountains, to the south, of the plains. Occasionally an eagle swam through this clear unobstructed mass of light and air. That was all.

And Carignano, her home on the ridge, had no more than that. Why should it? The sun shone on its white walls. Its windows were open – the ones facing north opened onto the blue waves of the Himalayas flowing out and up to the line of ice and snow sketched upon the sky, while those that faced south looked down the plunging cliff to the plain stretching out, flat and sere, to the blurred horizon.

Yes, there were some apricot trees close to the house. There were clumps of iris that had finished blooming. There was the kitchen with a wing of smoke lifting out of its chimney and a stack of wood outside its door. But these were incidental, almost unimportant. Nanda Kaul did not regard them very highly even if she stooped now to pick up a bright apricot from the short, dry grass. It had been squashed by its fall and she flung it away. Immediately, a bright hoopoe, seeing its flight and flash, struck down at it and tore at its bright flesh, then flew off with a lump in its beak. It had its nest in the eaves outside her bedroom window, she knew, but did not stay to watch the nestlings fed. It was a sight that did not fill her with delight. Their screams were shrill and could madden.

Instead she turned and climbed up the knoll, the topmost height of her garden, where the wind was keenest and the view widest.

4

But, on achieving it, she stopped to get her breath and glanced down just as the postman came out of a shadowed fold of the mountain onto the road below her gate. Still plodding on, dismally on, closer to Carignano. Her nostrils pinched and whitened with disapproval.

He slowed down, drawing out her irritation, keeping behind a small schoolboy who had materialized out of the hillside and was dawdling schoolwards without much sense of purpose or direction for he would stop now to pick up a flat stone, now to shy it at a chipmunk, then climb halfway up a hill for a thorny snatchful of raspberries, then slide down on his bottom into the ditch and search for a golden beetle. The postman seemed unable to overtake him – hypnotized by the boy's whimsical progress, he stopped and kept behind while Nanda Kaul, slit-eyed, burned on the knoll.

Hurry, man, she mentally snapped – get it over with.

Then, not being able to bear watching any more of such fantastic indecision, she turned around and gazed at her house instead, simple and white and shining on the bleached ridge. On the north side the wall was washed by the blue shadows of the low, dense apricot trees. On the east wall, the sun glared, scoured and sharp. It seemed so exactly right as a house for her, it satisfied her heart completely. How could it ever have belonged to anyone else? What could it possibly have been like before Nanda Kaul came to it? She could not imagine.

Chapter 2

The postman could imagine nothing but he knew a few things. He had known the house before it was Nanda Kaul's.

Not throughout its history, no, for it had been built in 1843, by a Colonel Macdougall, for his wife who could not bear the heat in the military cantonment at Ambala in the plains and hoped to save her ominously pale children by taking them to the mountains in the summer. So it says in his memoirs, which he had privately published and distributed but which are no longer available. He ended his account of his active life and the many military manoeuvres in which he had taken part with a description of this house he called Carignano and of how he and his wife Alice would sit by the window of an evening – she wrapped in a cashmere shawl for she was sickly and he with his pipe and tobacco – and gaze out across the valley to Sabathu where, amongst the white flecks of the gravestones in the military cemetery, their own seven children came to be buried, one by one.

The house stood empty for some years after the colonel and his wife Alice were themselves carried over the hills to the cemetery in Sabathu and, one day, during a terrific thunderstorm, nearly came to an end. The entire roof – sheets of corrugated iron that Colonel Macdougall had had painted green but that had eventually faded to its natural rusty grey – was lifted off the square stone walls and hurled down the hill as far as Garkhal where its sharp edge sliced the head off a coolie who was trying to shelter beside a load of stacked wood on the roadside.

Eventually the roof was replaced – but not the coolie's head – and the house taken by the pastor of Kasauli's one church. He found it sad that its exposed situation on the ridge made it impossible to plant the cottage garden he would have liked but he did plant three apricot trees where the house sheltered them from the worst gales, and they flourished in the stony soil and bore fruit. In his delight he bought a marble bird bath at a sale held at the Garden House whose owners, the aged sisters Abbott, died within a week

6

of each other and whose goods were auctioned off, and placed it under the trees. It was his joy to watch the bul-buls and hoopoes come to feast on the apricots and flutter down into the bird bath and plunge and preen and scatter the water in spray.

His joy would have been complete if his wife had made him apricot jam. But she would not. She hated him too much to cook jam for him. The longer their marriage the more she hated him and almost daily she made an attempt to murder him. But he survived. When she had her back turned he would pour out the tea she had brewed for him into a pot of geraniums beside his chair and silently watch them droop and die. He woke to see her the second before she plunged the kitchen knife into him and learnt to sleep with one eye open till he went blind – but that was after Mavis died: slipping on her way to the outdoor kitchen, she plunged down the cliff and split her head open on a rock, and so he lived on safely and died 'peacefully', as they say, in a bed in Lady Linlithgow's sanatorium for the tubercular. His ghost was said to haunt the house, or at least his pipe did, for at a certain moment of the evening the veranda would be wafted over by the rich, ripe odour of invisible tobacco freshly kindled.

The maiden lady who was the next occupant of the house, a Miss Appleby who had been governess in Lady Stuart's household and been left enough money to buy Carignano and so avoid the English climate for the rest of her life, certainly smelt that tobacco. Being used to the finest cheroots in the fine Stuart household, it would make her jump up and stamp her foot and yell with rage. The worst was that the ghost himself never appeared or Miss Appleby would surely have flung her entire willow pattern dinner set at him: her temper was famous. She once not only thrashed the gardener for planting marigolds which she hated – again, it was the smell she could not bear – but climbed onto

his back and whipped him around the garden, yelling
'No marigolds, understand? No marigolds in my garden!'

She was the first in the long line of maiden ladies who
inhabited Carignano – all English of course for in those days
all the houses along the Mall were owned by English people
and Indians were not so much as allowed to walk on the
Mall but were expected to keep to the footpaths on the hillsides and respectfully cast their eyes down when the English
sahibs and memsahibs cantered by on their horses. There
was a legend attached to each of these maiden ladies and the
postman knew a few of them.

There was a Miss Lawrence who had ridden across the
Thar desert wearing a linen hat and veil and perhaps fancy-
ing it was the Sahara. The two Misses Hughes – known
locally, and aptly, as the Misses Huges – had merely played
bridge at the club and made apricot jam that was famous
from Lawrence School at Sanawar to the military cantonment at Sabathu. They filled the house with chintz sofa-
covers and great china ewers and basins on which pink and
blue carnations mingled and that still minced and curtsied
about in the dank and mildewed bathrooms of Carignano.
They also planted a yellow rose creeper to climb the railing
that kept the house from rolling over the cliff down to the
plains. All year this creeper was a furry grey mass, stirring
and rustling as if it housed a colony of mice, but in April it
would exhale a billowing cloud of pale yellow roses – an
extravagance, a flamboyance, a largesse of roses, of creamy
yellow, of the scent of damp tea-leaves. Every year Nanda
Kaul stared at it in astonishment, wondering where all this
lacy, frilly prettiness came from in her hard, stony garden,
gale-blown and dour. It crept over the outdoor kitchen,
over the woodhouse, and trailed upon every rail, gate and
fence, sleeping and sighing all year but for that one month
when it was re-born like a sweet, angelic infant in pastel

8

frills and flounces. Then Nanda Kaul stopped to muse upon the Misses Hughes for a while.

After them, Miss Jane Shrewsbury brewed a more notorious stuff out of the things she grew or dug out of this garden – she said it cured scorpion bites and claimed to have saved many a stung villager carried up to her house, howling in agony. She also poked a fork into her cook's neck when he was choking on a mutton bone in the belief it would make an aperture for him to breathe through. Unfortunately he died and there was much scandal before Dr Hardy, the local medical lion, gave out that it was definitely the mutton bone that killed him and not the fork as suggested by the local scandal-mongers. That was in 1935 and two years later the lady herself was buried in the Kasauli graveyard under a tall cypress, and war broke out immediately thereafter.

During those war years a vivacious Miss Weaver and a reputedly promiscuous Miss Polson fluttered about Carignano in flowered dresses and picture hats, entertaining the Tommies to tea and sherry parties. They organized jumble sales and Saturday night dances at the club just below Carignano and it was the gayest time ever known in Kasauli, the closest Kasauli ever came to being Simla. Memsahibs sent up for the summer and Tommies sent to recuperate from the battlefields jigged and romped with an unknown abandon.

Suddenly it was all over. It was 1947. Maiden ladies were not thought to be safe here any more. Quickly, quickly, before the fateful declaration of independence, they were packed onto the last boats and shipped back to England – virginity intact, honour saved, natives kept at bay. A hefty sigh went up – of relief, of regret. A commonplace remark amongst them had been how like Kasauli was to English country towns of memory. Back in those English country towns, so unexpectedly and prematurely, they sighed and

9

said no, these were nothing like Kasauli, let alone Simla. But there was nothing to be done, no going back. Carignano was up for sale and Nanda Kaul bought it. The little town went native.

Chapter 3

When he came to the chestnut tree at the foot of the hill to which was nailed a signboard with CARIGNANO written on it in brass letters the postman suddenly came out of hypnosis, lost patience and gave an angry yell.

'Get on with you,' he shouted, raising his hand in threat. 'Past ten o'clock and you're still footling along the road.'

The boy gave a start and fled – instinctively, by reflex action. Having run part of the way downhill in surprise, he braked, stopped and, stooping quickly, picked a blade of grass, held it to his lips and gave a rude blast on it to show the postman what he thought of his sudden interference. Then, whistling pleasantly, he hopped erratically on, his large khaki shorts lolloping about his thin hips and his dusty hair flopping up and down on his small head.

Coming up the hill from the direction of the bazaar was Ram Lal, the Carignano cook, carrying a market bag in which a marrow, a loaf of bread and a minced mass of mutton were squashed together in the heat. Ram Lal walked slowly, staring at his tennis shoes which were a size too large for him and sank into the white dust, making a chain of craters for idle dogs to investigate.

Seeing him approach, the postman sank down on a bit of wall under the leafy chestnut tree. He would walk up the steep hill to the house with Ram Lal for company. He shifted the bag of letters on his shoulder. It was the first really hot day in May and he was sweating. He could have handed the single letter to Ram Lal to take up to the house, but he wiped his forehead with his finger and resolved not to do so, hot as he was. The postman had served in the army for fifteen years before he was discharged and entered the postal service, and he lived rigidly according to rule, as though there were still a sergeant-major behind him, shouting orders whenever he stopped, getting him to move on, punctually and obediently. The postman's ideal was the donkey and he lived like one and sat and waited for Ram Lal to come flopping from crater to crater along the dusty road. At least he would have him for company up that last back-breaking bit to Carignano.

Not that Ram Lal was much company. He was as stiff, almost, as the postman and every bit as dour. When he found the postman waiting for him in the shade of the chestnut tree, all he did was grunt and pause long enough to move the market bag from his right hand to his left.

The postman grunted in answer and got up, heaving his postbag over his shoulder once more.

The pony man went by in a comfortable clatter, leading his pony by the head, a small blonde child from the hotel on its back, and waved his arm and hallooed to the two men. They gave him identical looks of grudging recognition and disapproval of his carefree, clattering ways, grunted in unison and began the climb. The pony man went whistling on, waving a wand he had cut from a bush of Spanish broom. The blonde child nodded involuntarily, sun-struck.

Together, bent-backed, they toiled up the steep path, stones slipping from under their feet, in a way that wildly irritated Nanda Kaul who had come down from the knoll to wait for the postman at the gate, for she always made a point of keeping her back as straight as a rod when walking up that path.

11

Sighting her, grey and only faintly stirring under the three pine trees that stood by the gate in their exaggerated attitudes as of men going up in flames with their arms outstretched, charred, too, about the trunks, the postman felt something ominous hover in the heavy summer light and mumbled to Ram Lal, 'No visitors yet?'

Ram Lal merely shook his head.

The postman gave a snorting laugh. Ram Lal turned to stare at him with his small, red-streaked eyes. The postman immediately looked apologetic. 'Every house in Kasauli is bursting now,' he explained. 'It is the season.'

'We have none,' said Ram Lal, firmly.

At the gate, they parted. The postman stood shuffling through his letters and Ram Lal, slightly ducking his capped head to Nanda Kaul, went past her to the kitchen where great, bony, dusty chickens sprang down from the stack of wood by the door to greet him. He flapped at them with his market bag and they croaked back in alarm but crowded closer. They were said to be the descendants of Miss Jane Shrewsbury's original poultry and certainly looked antique, hardy. When he had disappeared into the smoky gloom of the kitchen, they crowded about the door, scraping the floor with their crooked toes in an excited scrabble for attention. In a while he started flinging chopped vegetable heads at them, each one accompanied by a word of filthy abuse.

In the meantime, the postman had detached one letter from the rest and silently handed it over to Nanda Kaul who said clearly but in a voice of suffering, 'Thank you.' Holding it with her fingers, at a little distance from her side, she walked slowly up the flagstone path along which day lilies bloomed desultorily, under the apricot trees to the veranda where she had her old cane chair.

Here was a letter and she would have to open it. She

12

resolved to say 'No' to whatever demand or request it contained. No, no, no.

Chapter 4

The veranda lay deep in shade. The tiles of its uneven floor were cool. Along the stone steps were pots of geraniums and fuchsias that bloomed unimpaired by the sun as they stood in the shade cast by the low, leafy apricot trees. Here was her old cane chair and she sat down on it, putting the letter down on her lap and gazing instead at the ripening apricots and the pair of bul-buls that quarrelled over them till they fell in a flurry of feathers to the ground, stirred up a small frenzy of dust, then shot off in opposite directions, scolding and abusing till a twist of a worm distracted them. Then there were only the cicadas to be heard, a sound so even and so insubstantial that it seemed to emerge from the earth itself, or from the season – a scent of pine-needles made audible, a spinning of sunlight or of the globe on its axis.

Looking past the leafy branches of those trees and the silvery needles of the pines at the gate, she could see the red rooftops of Lawrence School on the hilltop across the valley, and the fine spire of its church emerging from the seclusion of Sanawar's greenery. It was a comfortable view to have from one's veranda – more comfortable than the one from the back windows of the cliff plunging seven thousand feet down to the Punjab plains – but she was not comforted.

She looked at the scene with her accustomed intensity till a large white and yellow butterfly crossed over, disturbing her concentration, and made her look down at the letter.

It was addressed in her daughter's handwriting. The least loved or, at any rate, the most exasperating of her daughters. Asha, the beauty, had dedicated her life to the cultivation of long, glossy hair and an unwrinkled skin and had had little time left over for her unfortunate daughter, the one who married a diplomat and, as a result of his ill treatment of her, the affairs he had, his drinking and brutality, was reduced to a helpless jelly, put away out of sight and treated as an embarrassment who could, if she tried, pull herself together. In her last letter Asha had written, with her usual heartless blitheness, that she had persuaded Tara to try again. Tara's husband was given a new posting, this time in Geneva, and Asha had persuaded her daughter to go with him, to give him another chance. There was the little problem of their child who was only just recovering from a near-fatal attack of typhoid, but Asha was sure they would find a way to deal with this minor problem. The main thing, she had trumpeted, was for Tara to rouse herself and make another try at being a successful diplomat's wife. Surely Geneva would be an excellent place for such an effort. 'Why, why shouldn't she be happy?' Asha had written and Nanda Kaul had not replied, had been too disgusted to reply.

She felt an enormous reluctance to open this letter. She looked at it with distaste and foreboding for a long time before she finally tore it open and drew out the bundle of dark blue pages across which Asha's large writing pranced. This writing had none of the writer's loveliness – it sprawled and spread and shrieked out loud an aggressive assurance and aplomb.

In this writing she conveyed a series of disasters and tragedies to her mother who read it through with her lips pressed so tightly together that it made deep lines furrow the skin from the corners of her nostrils to the corners of her mouth, dark runnels of disapproval.

'Darling Mama' (wrote Asha, and Nanda Kaul could scarcely believe that there had been a time when she was actually addressed as such and heard it quite naturally and calmly), 'just a note this time as I'm in a mad rush. Now that I've persuaded Tara into going to Geneva and Rakesh into taking her – one day I'll tell you how I did that, I had a long talk with him, he's not really so bad as Tara might make you believe, she simply doesn't understand him, doesn't understand *men*, and she really is the wrong type of wife for a man like him so I can't blame him *entirely* although it is true that he does drink – well, I have to get Tara ready. This last year she's done *nothing*, Mama, just let herself go to rack and ruin, as well as her house – and poor little Raka, as you well know. Now she depends on me to wind up her household here and prepare her things and do her shopping for her – she says *she* can't, all she does is sit by Raka's bed and read her stories. So it's poor me who has to dash about all over Delhi – in the heat and dust-storms of summer – buying her saris, jewellery, getting her blouses tailored, having her suitcases mended, everything! Well, I mustn't complain, Mama, you know all I want is Tara to be happy and lead a good life. So I am doing all this for her without complaining.

'But there is one problem I can't help Tara with' (the letter ran on just as Nanda Kaul had known it would, and she tensed her knees under the silk folds of her sari) 'and the problem is, of course, Raka. Now, Mama, you know I have to dash off to Bombay at the end of the month to help Vina with her confinement – you see how old grandmothers have to rush about these days, it's almost as bad as having another set of babies oneself – and Tara thought I could take Raka with me. But that is quite out of the question. Poor little Raka looks like a ghost and hasn't quite got over her typhoid yet. She is very weak and the heat and humidity of Bombay will do her no good. Everyone who sees her says

15

she should go to the hills to recuperate. So Tara and I have decided it will be best to send her to you for the summer. Later, when Tara is settled in Geneva and has set up house, she will send for Raka. At the moment it is not possible for the child to travel or live in an hotel. We can't think of a better way for her to recuperate than spend a quiet summer with you in Kasauli. And I know how happy it will make you to have your great-grandchild for company in that lonely house' (here Asha's writing, bloated with self-confidence, doubled in size and fairly swelled up out of the blue paper at Nanda Kaul). 'Now Rakesh's brother has very kindly agreed to take Raka with him as far as Kalka – he's taking his family to Simla for a short holiday and Raka can travel with them as far as Kalka. There, he will put her in a taxi and send her up to Kasauli. It should be quite safe. She will be with you on . . .'

Nanda Kaul narrowed her eyes as she went over the details of her great-grandchild's journey. Then she folded the blue sheets firmly, as if suppressing the hurry and rush of her daughter's excited plans, and slipped them back into the envelope. Placing it on her lap again, she looked out into the apricot trees, down the path to the gate, the cloudy hydrangeas, the pines scattering and hissing in the breeze, to the red roofs of Lawrence School on Sanawar's green hilltop. One long finger moved like a searching insect over the letter on her lap, moved involuntarily as she struggled to suppress her anger, her disappointment and her total loathing of her daughter's meddling, busybody ways, her granddaughter's abject helplessness, and her great-granddaughter's impending arrival here at Carignano.

She tried to divert her mind from these thoughts and concentrate on this well known and perpetually soothing scene. She tried to look on it as she had before the letter arrived, with pleasure and satisfaction. But she was too distracted now.

All she wanted was to be alone, to have Carignano to herself, in this period of her life when stillness and calm were all that she wished to entertain.

Chapter 5

Getting up at last, she went slowly round to the back of the house and leant on the wooden railing on which the yellow rose creeper had blossomed so youthfully last month but was now reduced to an exhausted mass of grey creaks and groans again. She gazed down the gorge with its gashes of red earth, its rocks and gullies and sharply spiked agaves, to the Punjab plains – a silver haze in the summer heat – stretching out to a dim yellow horizon, and said Is it wrong? Have I not done enough and had enough? I want no more. I want nothing. Can I not be left with nothing? But there was no answer and of course she expected none.

Looking down, over all those years she had survived and borne, she saw them, not bare and shining as the plains below, but like the gorge, cluttered, choked and blackened with the heads of children and grandchildren, servants and guests, all restlessly surging, clamouring about her.

She thought of the veranda of their house in the small university town in Punjab, the Vice-Chancellor's house over which she had presided with such an air as to strike awe into visitors who came to call and leave them slightly gaping. She had had her cane chair there, too, and she had sat there, not still and emptily, but mending clothes, sewing on strings and buttons and letting out hems, at her feet a small charcoal brazier on which a pot of *kheer* bubbled, snipping threads and instructing the servant girl to stir, stir, don't stop stirring or it'll burn, and then someone had to be called to hold the smallest child from falling into the bubbling pot and carry it away, screaming worse than if it were scalded. Into this din, a tonga had driven up and disgorged a flurry of guests in their visiting saris, all to flap their palm-leaf hand-fans as they sat in a ring about her – the wives and daughters of the lecturers and professors over whom her husband ruled. She thought of that hubbub and of how she had managed and how everyone had said, pretending to think she couldn't hear but really wanting her to, 'Isn't she splendid? Isn't she like a queen? Really, Vice-Chancellor is lucky to have a wife who can run everything as she does,' and her eyes had flashed when she heard, like a pair of black blades, wanting to cut them, despising them, crawling grey bugs about her fastidious feet. That was the look no one had dared catch or return.

Looking down at her knuckles, two rows of yellow bones on the railing, she thought of her sons and daughters, of her confinements, some in great discomfort at home and others at the small filthy missionary-run hospital in the bazaar, and the different nurses and doctors who had wanted to help her but never could, and the slovenly, neurotic ayahs she had had to have because there was such a deal of washing and ironing to do and Mr Kaul had wanted her always in silk, at the head of the long rosewood table in the dining-room, entertaining his guests.

Mentally she stalked through the rooms of that house – his house, never hers – very carefully closing the wire-screen doors behind her to keep out the flies, looking sharply to see if the dark furniture, all rosewood, had been polished and the doors of the gigantic cupboards properly shut. She sniffed to make sure the cook was not smoking *biris* in the kitchen and to verify that all the metalware smelt freshly of Brasso.

She seemed to hear poignant shrieks from the canna beds

18

in the garden – a child had tumbled off the swing, another had been stung by a wasp, a third slapped by the fourth – and gone out on the veranda to see them come wailing up the steps with cut lips, bruised knees, broken teeth and tears, and bent over them with that still, ironic bow to duty that no one had noticed or defined.

Now, to bow again, to let that noose slip once more round her neck that she had thought was freed fully, finally. Now to have those wails and bawls shatter and rip her still house to pieces, to clutter the bare rooms and the cool tiles with the mountainous paraphernalia that each child seems to require or anyway demand. Now to converse again when it was silence she wished, to question and follow up and make sure of another's life and comfort and order, to involve oneself, to involve another.

It seemed hard, it seemed unfair, when all she wanted was the sound of the cicadas and the pines, the sight of this gorge plunging, blood-red, down to the silver plain.

An eagle swept over it, far below her, a thousand feet below, its wings outspread, gliding on currents of air without once moving its great muscular wings which remained in repose, in control. She had wished, it occurred to her, to imitate that eagle – gliding, with eyes closed.

Then a cuckoo called, quite close, here in her garden, very softly, very musically, but definitely calling – she recognized its domestic tone.

She gave that ironic bow again, very, very slightly, and went to the kitchen to see what Ram Lal had for her lunch and tell him about the great-grandchild's visit.

He blinked rather nervously, she thought.

Chapter 6

When she was back on her cane chair on the veranda, watching the sunlight spread over the tiles like a bright lacquer – too bright, too dry – the telephone rang. It rang so seldom, at Carignano, that its ringing sounded extraordinary, ominous.

Sitting bolt upright in her chair and trembling slightly, Nanda Kaul pressed the palms of her hands together and wondered whether to punish it by letting it ring itself to death or end her agony by answering it quickly. Its persistent shrilling was so painful that she was obliged to do the latter which seemed to her like a weakness, offending her still further.

She held the black ear-phone awkwardly, resenting its uncomfortable pressure on the small bones of her ear, picked surlily at the pages of the telephone directory and stared out of the window at a large hen scratching under the hydrangea. The look on her face was one no one had ever caught on it – she had allowed no one to, ever.

A burst of crackling and hissing, as of suddenly awakened geese, a brief silence, then a voice issued from it that made her gasp and shrivel, balling up her fingers tightly. The voice was not merely shrill, not merely strident, it was shrill and strident as no other voice ever was but Ila Das's.

Moving the ear-phone a few safe inches away from her ear, Nanda Kaul sighed resignedly. She knew this voice was Ila Das's tragedy in life and wondered, as always when she heard it, if Ila Das herself knew it. They had been together in school and college and from that time to this there had been no hint that Ila Das might harbour such a devastating suspicion about herself.

The shock of that hideous voice made it impossible to follow what was being said for a minute or two.

'Where are you speaking from, Ila?' she asked when there was a small pause in the piping, shrilling screech that was poor Ila's speech, like a long nail frantically scratching at a glass pane, or a small child gone berserk and prattling on and on in a voice no one could hear without cringing.

'I'm lunching at the sanatorium with the matron, my dear,' screamed Ila Das, 'and I thought, how nice, now I can make a few phone calls and get in touch with my friends. You know, I hardly ever get away from my village – it keeps me *sooo* busy, I never get a minute . . .' she babbled on and Nanda Kaul turned her head this way and that in an effort to escape. She watched the white hen drag out a worm inch by resisting inch from the ground till it snapped in two. She felt like the worm herself, she winced at its mutilation.

'And when can I come and see you?' screeched Ila Das. 'We haven't met for *ages*, dear, and I've so much to tell, I've been so busy, I must tell you all . . .'

'Yes,' sighed Nanda Kaul into the phone, her voice as pale as her face, 'but my great-granddaughter is coming to stay at the end of the week. I'm a bit busy myself, getting a room ready for her and so on . . .'

'But, Nanda, how *marvellous*,' the voice shrilled, achieving a new pitch, and it was not impossible, thought Nanda Kaul, that Ila was jumping up and down on her two feet in excitement. 'Your *great*-granddaughter did you say, Nanda? How marvellous, how – I must come and see her. At once! May I? May I, Nanda?'

Nanda Kaul's face seemed about to crack. It was cut from end to end with black furrows of desperation. She pressed her hand to her forehead and found it clammy. Her voice dropped lower and lower as she dropped words like small, cold pebbles into the mouthpiece. 'Yes, Ila, you must come – but wait a bit – when the child is settled, I'll let you know, I'll write you a note,' and quickly she put the phone down.

Still staring at the hen which was greedily gulping down bits of worm, she thought of her husband's face and the way he would plait his fingers across his stomach and slip heavy lids down over his eyes whenever Ila Das came, bobbing and bouncing, in button boots, her umbrella wildly swirling, to tea. The memory of his face, his expression, made her lips twist almost into a smile.

At the other end, Ila Das put down the sudden silence to nothing more unusual than an accidental cutting of the line, but she also wondered if there really had been a total lack of joy in Nanda Kaul's voice when she spoke of her great-grandchild's visit, if there really had been nothing in her voice beyond annoyance and apprehension, or if she had only imagined it. Fingering a yellowed curl, Ila Das hummed and wondered for a minute.

Chapter 7

The sunlight thickened. No longer lacquer, it turned to glue. Flies, too lazy for flight, were caught in its midday web and buzzed languorously, voluptuously, slowly unsticking their feet and crawling across the ceilings, the windowpanes, the varnished furniture. Inside, the flies. Outside, the cicadas. Everything hummed, shrilled, buzzed and fiddled till the strange rasping music seemed to materialize out of the air itself, or the heat.

Nanda Kaul lay on her bed, absolutely still, composing

her hands upon her chest, shutting her eyes to the brightness of the window, waiting for the first cool stir of breeze in the late afternoon to revive her. Till it came, she would lie still, still – she would be a charred tree trunk in the forest, a broken pillar of marble in the desert, a lizard on a stone wall. A tree trunk could not harbour irritation, nor a pillar annoyance. She would imitate death, like a lizard. No one would dare rouse her. Who would dare?

The parrots dared. A sudden quarrel broke out in the tree-tops, for a moment they all screamed and scolded together, then shot off like rockets, scattering pine nuts, disappearing into the light, disintegrating in the heat.

Then the stillness drew together, like glue drying in the sun, congealed, gathered weight, became lead. The heat had actual weight, she felt it on her chest, rising and falling with her slow breath. She groaned under it, very softly, and kept her eyes shut.

She had practised this stillness, this composure, for years, for an hour every afternoon: it was an art, not easily acquired. The most difficult had been those years in that busy house where doors were never shut, and feet flew, or tramped, without ceasing. She remembered how she had tried to shut out sound by shutting out light, how she had spent the sleepless hour making out the direction from which a shout came, or a burst of giggles, an ominous growling from the dogs, the spray of gravel under bicycle wheels on the drive, a contest of squirrels over the guavas in the orchard, the dry rattle of eucalyptus leaves in the sun, a drop, then spray and rush of water from a tap. All was subdued, but nothing was ever still.

From all sides these sounds invaded her room which was in the centre, and neither the wire gauze screens at the windows nor the striped Orissa cotton curtains at the doors kept them out. Everyone in the house knew it was her hour of rest, that she was not to be disturbed. She could hear a

23

half-asleep ayah hiss at the babies 'Quiet, go to sleep, you'll wake your mother.' She could hear her husband tell someone in a carefully lowered voice 'Later, I'll have to consult my wife about it. I'll let you know later.' She could hear her sons tiptoe past in their great, creaking boots, then fling their satchels down with a crash.

This would go on for an hour and she would keep her eyes tightly clenched, her hands folded on her chest – under a quilt in winter, or uncovered to the sullen breeze of the fan in summer – determinedly not responding. The effort not to respond would grow longer by the minute, heavier, more unendurable, till at last it was sitting on her chest, grasping her by the neck. At four o'clock she would break out from under it with a gasp. All right, she would say, sitting up on the edge of her bed and letting down her feet to search for her slippers, then straightening her hair – all right, she'd sigh, come, come all of you, get me, I'm yours, yours again.

She would barely have splashed her face with some water and combed out her hair when the baby would come crawling in, the first to hear her stir, the most insistent in its needs. Lifting it into her arms, she would go to the kitchen to see the milk taken out of the ice-box, the layer of cream drawn off, the row of mugs on a tray filled and carried out to the green table on the veranda around which the children already sat on their low cane stools – the little girls still having their long hair plaited and their fresh cotton dresses buttoned, and the boys throwing themselves backwards and kicking the table legs and clamouring with hunger. Then there was the bread to be spread with butter, jam jars opened and dug into, knives taken away from babies and boys, girls questioned about homework, servants summoned to mop up spilt milk and fetch tea, and life would swirl on again, in an eddy, a whirlpool of which she was the still, fixed eye in the centre.

Had they never been silent? Never absent? Plaiting her fingers together, contracting her eyelids, she fretted to catch at a saving memory, one that did not distract and hustle but cooled and calmed.

It seemed to her there had been an evening, or perhaps it was a night, certainly it was dark, and it was spring when only the evenings were cool and the last of the phlox bloomed in a border edging the lawn, close and white and fresh in the moonlight, giving out a scent of freshness and cool as she stepped onto the crisp grass of the lawn. Cool, yes, she had to wrap her arms about herself as she paced the lawn, almost walking into the badminton net that hung so grey and spidery as to be invisible in the ghostly light. Stepping back, she had walked around the badminton pole, along the line of lime dribbled over the close, dry grass, and stepped over a broken shuttlecock discarded beside a bed of white petunias over which moths fluttered in a kind of frantic ecstasy.

There had been badminton earlier in the day – not the children, but teachers, friends from the campus, had come to play. Now they had gone. The court was deserted. A waxen moon was climbing over the ghost-grey branches of the eucalyptus trees along the drive, eerily silent. There was a mingled odour of grass, of phlox, of eucalyptus leaves along with lime, sweat-soaked sports clothes, catgut and clammy tennis shoes. She sniffed at it with pinched nostrils, finding it offensive, lacking in composition and harmony.

Walking faster and faster back and forth, back and forth over the lawn, she had stayed out till she heard the car, an aged maroon Rover, turn in at the gate, seen its yellow headlights sweep over the quisqualis creeper that festooned the porch and light up the white pillars of the veranda, the beds of phlox and the uneven line of lime on the lawn. Lights off, silence, then the throwing open of the car door, and her husband had come out. He had been to drop some

25

of the guests home – no, she corrected herself with asperity, *one* of the guests home. She watched him go up the veranda steps, puffing at his cigar, and smelt the rich tobacco. She had stood very still in the shadow flung by the loqat tree in the corner of the lawn. She had not moved, not made a sound. She had watched him cross the veranda, go into the drawing-room, and waited till the light there went out and another came on in the bedroom that had been only a small dressing-room till she had had his bed put there. Then she paced the lawn again, slower and slower.

A lapwing started up in the mustard fields beyond the garden hedge, and rose, crying, in the air. That nervous, agitated bird, thought Nanda Kaul, watching its uneven flapping flight through the funereal moonlight, what made it leap so in fright, descend again on nervous feet, only to squawk and take off once more, making the night ring with its cries? That hunted, fearful bird, distracted and disturbing.

Herself a grey cat, a night prowler, she watched it till it disappeared in the direction of the river, its cries growing fainter. Then, rubbing her foot in the grass, she relished the sensation of being alone again.

That was one time she had been alone: a moment of private triumph, cold and proud.

The memory of it cast a shadow across her – it was cool. It made her stir, raise her hands to her cheeks, her hair, then slowly sit up. From the window the first breeze of late afternoon came wandering gently in, swinging the curtain with a dancer's movement.

She went to the window and looked out on the flushed ravine, the molten plains, the sky filled with a soft, tawny light in which the sun floated like a lighted balloon, making the pine-needles glisten like silk, like floss. It was time for tea.

26

Chapter 8

Seated on the veranda in the late afternoon shade, Nanda
Kaul waved away the tea tray and read, in small sips, bits
and pieces from *The Pillow Book of Sei Shonagon*.

When A Woman Lives Alone was the title of one scrap
that caught her eye:

> 'When a woman lives alone, her house should be
> extremely dilapidated, the mud wall should be falling to
> pieces, and if there is a pond, it should be overgrown with
> water plants. It is not essential that the garden be covered
> with sage-brush, but weeds should be growing through
> the sand in patches, for this gives the place a poignantly
> desolate look.
>
> 'I greatly dislike a woman's house when it is clear she
> has scurried about with a knowing look on her face,
> arranging everything just as it should be, and when the
> gate is kept tightly shut.'

Nanda Kaul looked up with a faint smile, then bent her
head to read it over again. Each time it went down her
throat with a clear, luminous passage, like chilled dry wine.

The afternoon light had softened. After a while, she went
out into the garden, still holding the book in her hand,
down to the three pines at the gate.

The hills were still sunlit, but the light was hazy, pow-
dery. They seemed to be covered with a golden fuzz and
melted into soft blues and violets in the distance.

She wished, as often before, that she could invite an

English water-colourist of the nineteenth century to come and paint the view from her garden. They were masters, she felt, at conveying light and space, the two elements of the Kasauli view. Or was it too unsubstantial a scene for an English artist? she wondered. No Indian artist of any epoch could have painted it, she knew, and she had her doubts about the English. She had seen nineteenth-century lithographs of what were then known as the Kussowlie Hills and although they had amused her, they had not satisfied. Perhaps a firmer outline, a more definite horizon was required by an etcher. Here hills melted into sky, sky into snows, snows into air.

She leaned over the gate, musing, her eyes resting on the hillsides mauve and violet in what her husband, a scholarly man who read many languages, had liked to call the *Abendleuchtung*. Cattle browsed homewards to small hidden hamlets in the valleys, all grew softer and greyer till it was quite dark and lights came out where she had not thought there was any habitation at all – single lamps here and there in Kasauli, pinpricks of light for Sanawar, little pools of blurred light for Sabathu and Dagshai and, far away in the distance, the pale fairy shimmer that was Simla.

The crickets fell silent. The wind dropped. She turned and went slowly in to find the light on in the small drawing-room. She sat reading Sei Shonagon's lists of Wind Instruments, Things that Give a Clean Feeling, Things That Give An Unclean Feeling, Things That Have Lost Their Power ('a boat which is high and dry in a creek at ebb-tide. A large tree that has been blown down in a gale and lies on its side with its roots in the air.'), Awkward Things, Things That Lose By Being Painted ('pinks, cherry blossom, yellow roses'), Things That Gain By Being Painted ('Pines, Autumn Fields. Mountain villages and paths. Cranes and deer.'), Herbs and Shrubs, Insects, Elegant Things, Birds, Trees and Festivals, and found herself spinning out lists of her own.

Then she returned to the passage about the woman who lived alone and smiled again, in spite of herself, wondering if Carignano would live up to that epicurean lady's ideas of how things should be. Not quite, for it was not desolate and it was not derelict. But she had an idea that its sparseness, its cleanness and austerity would please the Japanese lady of a thousand years ago as it pleased her.

The old house, the full house, of that period of her life when she was the Vice-Chancellor's wife and at the hub of a small but intense and busy world, had not pleased her. Its crowding had stifled her.

There had been too many trees in the garden – dark, dusty guava and mango trees, full of too many marauding parrots and squirrels and children that raided them for fruit and either over-ate or fell from the tops.

There had been too many servants in the long low row of whitewashed huts behind the kitchen, so that the drains often choked and overflowed, and the nights were loud with the sounds of festive drumming, of drunken singing and brawling, of bathing and washing and wailing children.

There had been too many guests coming and going, tongas and rickshaws piled up under the eucalyptus trees and the bougainvilleas, their drivers asleep on the seats with their feet hanging over the bars. The many rooms of the house had always been full, extra beds would have had to be made up, often in not very private corners of the hall or veranda, so that there was a shortage of privacy that vexed her. Too many trays of tea would have to be made and carried to her husband's study, to her mother-in-law's bedroom, to the veranda that was the gathering-place for all, at all times of the day. Too many meals, too many dishes on the table, too much to wash up after.

They had had so many children, they had gone to so

many different schools and colleges at different times of the day, and had so many tutors – one for mathematics who was harsh and slapped the unruly boys, one for drawing who was lazy and smiled and did nothing, and others equally incompetent and irritating. Then there had been their friends, all of different ages and sizes and families.

She had suffered from the nimiety, the disorder, the fluctuating and unpredictable excess.

She had been so glad when it was over. She had been glad to leave it all behind, in the plains, like a great, heavy, difficult book that she had read through and was not required to read again.

Would Raka's coming mean the opening of that old, troublesome ledger again?

Sighing, she went off to bed, dragging one foot uncharacteristically.

Discharge me, she groaned. I've discharged all my duties. Discharge.

Chapter 9

The care of others was a habit Nanda Kaul had mislaid. It had been a religious calling she had believed in till she found it fake. It had been a vocation that one day went dull and drought-struck as though its life-spring had dried up.

It had happened on her first day alone at Carignano. After her husband's death, her sons and daughters had come to help her empty the Vice-Chancellor's house, pack and crate their belongings and distribute them, then escort her to Kasauli. For a while, they had stood about, in Carignano, like too much furniture. She had wondered what to do with them.

Fortunately, they had gone away. Brought up by her to be busy and responsible, they all had families and employments to tend. None could stay with her. When they left, she paced the house, proprietorially, feeling the feel of each stone in the paving with bare feet.

She had drifted about the garden. Unlike any other owner of house and garden, she had not said: Here I will plant a willow, there I will pull out the Spanish broom and put in pampas grass instead. No, she revelled in its bareness, its emptiness. The loose pebbles of the gravel pleased her as much as rich turf might another. She cared not to add another tree to the group of apricots by the veranda or the group of three pines at the gate.

Like her, the garden seemed to have arrived, simply by a process of age, of withering away and an elimination, at a state of elegant perfection. It was made up of a very few elements, but they were exact and germane as the strokes in a Japanese scroll. She no more wished to add to them than she wished to add to her own pared, reduced and radiantly single life.

She could no more picture a child – a new, additional child – in this perfected and natural setting than she could a pergola of roses, a marble faun or a fountain. She wished for none of these. On the contrary, the thought of them sickened as a box of sweets might sicken.

In distress and agitation, she walked out to the kitchen to speak to Ram Lal when he returned from his daily expedition to the bazaar. As he sorted potatoes and onions on the wooden tabletop, she spoke to him with a nervousness that alarmed him as a thunderstorm in the air might have alarmed him.

'My great-granddaughter will be arriving tomorrow, Ram Lal,' she began, and her hands clung to each other and sweated.

'Yes,' he agreed, trying to sound reassuring, but failing.

'What will you cook for her, Ram Lal?' she asked, curiously troubled. It was as if she had never made up handsome dinner parties for fifty or seventy guests on Convocation Day, and been praised for the brilliance of the kebabs she served, or the richness of the puddings. So many scraps of paper, she had torn them up and thrown them away. She had lost the ample book with its frills and cuttings from magazines and papers of recipes with which to please and comfort her large family. Now not one idea remained, not one, with which to feed a single small great-granddaughter.

The amount she had jettisoned from her life might take another's breath away.

'What shall I make, Memsahib?' mumbled Ram Lal, his eyes downcast.

'I don't know, Ram Lal, I don't know,' she sighed, and suddenly clutched the edge of the table. 'Tell me. Suggest something.'

As suddenly, he looked up and inspiration gleamed in his bloodshot eyes. 'Potato chips, Memsahib,' he trumpeted. 'All children like potato chips.'

'Do they?' she murmured, and gazed at him with a dazed kind of hope that the potato chips might surfeit the child, lull it into a decent stranger and render it harmless.

'Yes, potato chips they like, with ketchup.'

'With . . .'

'Ketchup, Memsahib, tomato ketchup. I will buy a bottle from the bazaar. I will make it for lunch. Will she be here for lunch?'

'Yes,' nodded Nanda Kaul sadly, and moved towards the door, trying hard to cling to the vision of potato chips and tomato ketchup as the saving of them all. They sounded so cheerful but also, she had to admit, somehow inadequate.

Ram Lal went back to sorting potatoes and onions with a fresh vigour, but kept a wary eye on the Memsahib as she trailed back to the house over the gravel and pine-needles, with a new hesitation in her normally sure step. 'Old, old,' he muttered, when she was out of earshot, in the shade of the apricot trees. 'She is old, I am old. We are old, old,' he muttered, quickly losing hope.

A bony hen poked its neck in at the door and squawked in a particularly demanding and raucous tone. He flung his filthy market-bag at it in rage and it flew up onto the woodpile and stared at him with a surprised yellow eye.

Chapter 10

She did not, after all, walk down to the taxi-stand to meet Raka. She sent Ram Lal instead. She knew she ought to go. She knew if she took the road very slowly, gave it plenty of time, and carried a sunshade, she could do it. But she could not bear the thought of curious eyes that would see her, the loose mouths that would turn to each other and flap questioningly.

She stayed back, going into the guest room again and again to pick at the linen duchess set on the chest of drawers, drag open the cupboard doors and sniff at the damp, green smell of mould, pat the mattress and feel the hairy prickles through the smooth sheet.

She considered filling a vase with flowers and placing it beside the bed. But, when she went to the window and looked out, she saw only such flowers as succeed outdoors, not one that might retain its shape or colour inside.

On her way to the door, she bumped her leg against the bed-post. The bump seemed to knock the air out of her lungs. Gasping, she limped away to her room, feeling slightly sick.

In her room, she pulled up the petticoat to examine her thigh. No, no broken bone protruded, but the pimpled pearl of flesh was already turning into a rainbow-tinted bruise. Blue now, it would be violet tomorrow, green thereafter till it faded to yellow and then back to pearl. The putrid colours of old meat.

She groaned with self-pity and pain, certain that she was alone and no one would hear.

In an hour that privacy would be over. She could never groan aloud again: the child would hear.

Tenderly rubbing the bruise, she tried to distract her mind from the pain by remembering what she could of Raka. But now all the babies in her life ran together in one rainbow muddle – pinks, blues, bruises, bones – she could hardly separate her own from others. Was it Milon who had the ayah that fed him opium at night, under her fingernails, or was it Nikhil? Which of them, clinging to her knees, or lying dreamily with a head in her lap, had insisted 'When I grow big, you will grow small, and then I will look after you'? Could it have been Asha, the writer of those terrible letters? It could, for Asha had been a small girl with curls all over her head and a round, soft hand with which she had patted her mother when she had approved of her sari and jewels as she dressed before the mirror. 'When you are dead, I will get all your saris,' she had smugly said. That certainly sounded like Asha. But there were the others – her own and then the grandchildren. Recently it was Tara who had demanded the largest share of her sympathy and attention, with her unhappiness and her breakdowns. But the pregnant Vina, too, needed care. During her first pregnancy she had typhoid. Disaster-prone, during the second she had broken a leg and survived an attack of appendicitis. Asha's children appeared to attract all the tragedy that she herself had skirted with such complacent success. Now there was to be yet another great-grandchild. So how could she be

34

sure at which point in time Raka had arrived, in which city and hospital?

She had, in her time, embroidered so many muslin vests and cotton nightgowns, she could not recall if it was with a blue duck or a pink mouse that she had greeted Raka, whether she had sent a coral bracelet or a silver mug. It was not possible, groaned Nanda Kaul, when there were so many of them and they were as alike as human beings always are alike. She could not summon Raka out of the common blur. She was no more than a particularly dark and irksome spot on the hazy landscape – a mosquito, a cricket, or a grain of sand in the eye.

Hanging her head miserably, it seemed too much to her that she should now have to meet Raka, discover her as an individual and, worse, as a relation, a dependant. She would have to urge her to eat eggs and spinach, caution her against lifting stones in the garden under which scorpions might lie asleep, see her to bed at night and lie in the next room, wondering if the child slept, straining to catch a sound from the bedroom, their opposing thoughts colliding in the dark like jittery bats in flight.

She would never be able to sleep, Nanda Kaul moaned to herself, how could she sleep with someone else in the house? She was so unused to it, it would upset her so.

And she would have to order proper meals even though she herself wanted nothing but a piece of toast, apricots from the garden, that was all. Perhaps the child would be bored and need to be entertained? How would she do that? Once she had known nursery rhymes, word games, possessed skills with paper and cloth, pins and scissors – but they were all gone, buried under layers of dust, she had not the vitality to delve for them. Should she take the child for walks then? To the club? Should she invite other children to play? But she knew no one, certainly no children, in Kasauli. She had held herself religiously aloof, jealous of this privacy achieved only at the very end of her life.

There was only Ila Das who had followed her out of the past and still came to see her. Should Ila Das be invited to meet the child?

The very thought wrung a snort of disgust from Nanda Kaul. Then she dropped her petticoat, stood, looked vaguely about the room and limped out to the veranda.

It was very still. Ram Lal had left for the taxi-stand. Raka would soon be here.

On the knoll and at the gate the wind ruffled the pine-needles so that they glistened silver in the sunlight. A cuckoo sang in the chestnut tree down by the road, with its low, domestic call.

PART II

Raka comes to Carignano

PART II

Early Letters to Castagno

Chapter 1

Raka – what an utter misnomer, thought Nanda Kaul, standing under the apricot trees with her hands pressed together before her and watching the child come in through the gate where the pine trees stood bending and twisting extravagantly in the wind as though miming welcome in a modern satiric ballet.

Raka meant the moon, but this child was not round-faced, calm or radiant. As she shuffled up the garden path, silently following Ram Lal, with a sling bag weighing down one thin, sloping shoulder and her feet in old sandals heavy with dust, Nanda Kaul thought she looked like one of those dark crickets that leap up in fright but do not sing, or a mosquito, minute and fine, on thin, precarious legs.

But 'Raka' she nevertheless said, hoping somehow to relate the name to the child and wondering if she would ever get used to seeing this stranger in her garden.

Raka slowed down, dragged her foot, then came towards her great-grandmother with something despairing in her attitude, saying nothing. She sucked at the loose, curly elastic of an old, broken straw hat that drooped over her closely cropped head like a straw bag. She turned a pair of extravagantly large and somewhat bulging eyes about in a way that made the old lady feel more than ever her resemblance to an insect.

Turning those eyes about, Raka watched Ram Lal go up the veranda steps into the house with her case, his outsized tennis shoes alternately flopping and squeaking on the stone tiles. Turning slightly, she saw a scraggy-necked hen pecking beneath a bush of blue hydrangeas at some pieces of broken white china.

Then she raised her small, shorn head on its very thin and delicate neck and regarded the apricot trees, the veranda, Carignano. She listened to the wind in the pines and the cicadas all shrilling incessantly in the sun with her unfortunately large and protruding ears, and thought she had never before heard the voice of silence.

Then it was not possible to postpone the meeting any longer and both moved a step closer to each other and embraced because they felt they must. There was a sound of bones colliding. Each felt how bony, angular and unaccommodating the other was and they quickly separated.

'Child, how ill you have been!' Nanda Kaul exclaimed involuntarily, leaving her hand for a moment on the straight hard shield of the thin shoulder. 'How ill. How thin it's made you.'

Raka pulled at the slack elastic with some embarrassment and rolled her eyes around to follow the flight of the hoopoe that suddenly darted out of the tree. She saw the old lady who murmured at her as another pine tree, the grey sari a rock – all components of the bareness and stillness of the Carignano garden.

To Nanda Kaul she was still an intruder, an outsider, a mosquito flown up from the plains to tease and worry. With a blatant lack of warmth, she sighed 'Well, better come in,' and led her across the wavy tiles of the veranda to her room.

Chapter 2

Left to herself in the afternoon, Raka felt over the room with her bare feet. She walked about as the newly caged, the newly tamed wild ones do, sliding from wall to wall on silent, investigating pads. She patted a cheek of wood here, smoothed a ridge of plaster there. She met a spider that groomed its hairs in a corner, saw lizard's eyes blinking out of a dark groove. She probed the depth of dust on shelves and ledges, licked a windowpane to cool her tongue-tip. She sagged across the bed on her stomach, hung her head over its edge, but the sun caught her eye, slipped in its yellow wedge and would not allow her to close it.

It summoned her to the window, dragged her the length of a ray and drew her to the ledge where she laid her head on its comfortable guillotine.

Below the window she saw stones in a heap, flowers that held no interest, a snail's discarded shell. Not much.

But a few feet further on, under the hopeless wooden railing, lay the lip of the cliff and the sudden drop down the red, rock-spattered ravine to the plain that lay stretched out and heavy, the dusty pelt of a yellow animal panting in the sun. Raka blinked at it. She knew it – that plain, that pelt, that yellow summer dust.

Slipping one leg over the window sill, she climbed out into the bed of day lilies and went quietly to lean over the railing and look down. She knew her great-grandmother's window overlooked the same scene. She was careful not to crunch the pebbles under her feet. Crouching by the rail, she made out the details that gave the hazy scene edges, angles and interest.

Shoals of rusted tins, bundles of stained newspaper, peels, rags and bones, all snuggling in grooves, hollows, cracks, and sometimes spilling. Pine trees with charred trunks and contorted branches, striking melodramatic attitudes as on stage. Rocks arrested in mid-roll, rearing up, dropping. Occasional tin rooftops, glinting.

Looking down the length of the jagged ledge, Raka saw it lined with other back walls and servants' quarters, tin sheds and cook-houses. Around the bend, these grew in size, rose and billowed into the enormous concrete walls of what looked like a factory, for sharp chimneys thrust out cushions and scarves of smoke, black on the milky blue of the afternoon sky. Chutes emerging from its back wall seemed built to disgorge factory waste into the ravine and immediately below them were small, squat structures that looked like brick kilns amongst the spiked, curved blades of the giant agaves that were, besides the pines, the only vegetation of that blighted gorge.

Puzzled, Raka turned her head on its stalk, gently. Her father and grandmother had extolled the beauties and delights of a Himalayan hill-station to her, but said nothing of factories. Here was such an enormous one that Raka wondered at their ignorance of it. To her, it seemed to dominate the landscape – a square dragon, boxed, bricked and stoked.

Lizard-like, she clung to the rail and slid along its length to the outdoor kitchen and looked in to see if Ram Lal were there and could enlighten her. But the place was empty, a blackened, fire-blasted cave in which one fiery, inflamed eye glowed and smouldered by itself. A white hen that had insinuated itself into the kitchen unnoticed, saw the flutter of her white dress, squawked out loud and shot past her, making her step aside in surprise.

In the room next to the kitchen, still smaller but somewhat brightened by the myriad magazine and calendar pictures stuck to the smoky walls, Ram Lal lay on his string cot, his limbs flung out to its four corners, his cap on his nose, lifting and falling with the low growls and sudden snorts that came and went beneath it.

Leaving him, Raka detached herself from the kitchen walls and climbed the knoll that rose above the kitchen, helping herself up by holding onto fistfuls of hairy ferns and protruding rocks, to the top where pine trees grew in a ring amongst the stones. Here a breeze stirred, cool, dry and resinous.

Raka leaned against the crusted bark of the tree, as thick and scorched as pieces of burnt toast, feeling the cracked surfaces by rubbing her shoulder-blades against them. Down below her, on the other side of the knoll, was the green rooftop of a large, low building that had bright geraniums in baskets along its verandas, white muslin curtains that the windows alternately inhaled and exhaled, a giant deodar tree to shade it and, across the road, freshly swept and marked tennis courts, empty and waiting. That must be the club her grandmother had spoken of, but deserted now, asleep. It seemed that all Kasauli slept except for the cicadas that sawed and fiddled without stop. In the sky, huge vultures circled lazily, stealthily, on currents of air, prowling for game.

Raka slid down on her haunches, then lowered herself onto a flat stone at the foot of the tree. Resting the small knobs of her spine against the trunk, she surveyed Sanawar which lay in the deep shade of its trees, and Dagshai and Sabathu, handfuls of pebbles gleaming on golden hilltops. A cricket close by broke in raucously upon the silence and she spent the rest of the afternoon lifting stones in search of it.

Chapter 3

When at last she heard Ram Lal knocking about in the kitchen, making tea – the loose, jingling sounds so clearly proclaimed tea-time and not any other, heavier meal – she slid down the knoll and went to question him about the factory.

In between setting out the tea-cups on an old walnut tray, blowing up the fire into a blaze and whipping at clouds of smoke with his kitchen rags, Ram Lal told her.

'That is the Pasteur Institute. It is where doctors make serum for injections. When a man is bitten by a mad dog, he is taken there for injections – fourteen, in the stomach. I've had them myself. Once a whole village was rounded up and taken there – a dog had gone mad and bitten everyone in the village. The dog had to be killed. Its head was cut off and sent to the Institute. The doctors cut them open and look into them. They have rabbits and guinea pigs there, too, many animals. They use them for tests.'

He stopped to pour boiling water from the great black kettle into the tea-pot and Raka watched the hissing stream, hanging onto the edge of the table by her fingernails.

'Why is there so much smoke?' she asked, in a somewhat weak voice.

'Oh, they are always boiling serum there – boiling, boiling. They make serum for the whole country.'

Going out with the tea-tray balanced professionally on the palm of one hand, he stopped by the railing and nodded in the direction of the concrete Institute walls that had worried Raka by their incongruity and their oddly oppressive threat. 'See those chutes? They empty the bones and ashes of dead animals down into the ravine. It's a bad place. Don't go there.'

'Why?'

'Jackals come at night to chew the bones. Then they go mad and bite the village dogs. The mad dogs run around, biting people. Keep away from there, huh? Specially at night. At night you hear jackals howling and people have seen ghosts.' He lowered his voice. 'The ghosts of people who have died of dog-bite and snake-bite roam on the hillsides. It isn't safe, hear?'

Raka pressed pale lips together and nodded. She followed

44

Ram Lal to the veranda where he put down the tray, and sat down very stiff and still while her great-grandmother poured out a cup of milk for her with a drop of tea in it.

As she handed over the cup, Nanda Kaul narrowed her eyes and said 'How pale you are, child. Didn't you rest at all?'

Raka ducked her head and lifted the cup to her mouth. Her great-grandmother was left to interpret the motion as she wished.

After they had emptied their cups, 'What will you do with yourself now, Raka?' Nanda Kaul wondered, having watched the child seethe silently on the small stool beside her, seethe as if she were a thousand black mosquitoes, a stilly humming conglomerate of them, and did not know whether to contain or release this dire seething.

She chose not to. She did not want to be drawn into a child's world again – real or imaginary, it was bound to betray. Sighing under the weight of her destiny, she poured out another cup of hot, black tea, murmuring 'How hot it's grown. Too hot. Do you think you'd like to take a walk or is it too hot?' Let her contain herself or release herself, whatever she could do best, thought Nanda Kaul, drinking the bitter dregs.

Chapter 4

Nanda Kaul never discovered what Raka did with herself. All she discovered was that the child had a gift for disappearing – suddenly, silently. She would be gone, totally, not to return for hours.

Occasionally she caught a glimpse of her scrambling up a stony hillside, grasping at tufts of grass or bushes of Spanish broom, her small white-knickered bottom showing above a pair of desperately clinging heels. Or wandering down a lane in a slow, straying manner, stopping to strip a thorny bush of its few berries or to examine an insect under a leaf. Then she would round a boulder or drop from the lip of a cliff and vanish.

She would return with her brown legs scratched, her knees bruised, sucking a finger stung by nettles, her hair brown under a layer of dust, her eyes very still and thoughtful as though she had visited strange lands and seen fantastic, improbable things that lingered in the mind.

It was against the old lady's policy to question her but it annoyed her intensely that she should once again be drawn into a position where it was necessary for her to take an interest in another's activities and be responsible for their effect and outcome.

When would she be done?

She wrote a letter to Asha in her very plain, tall writing, in green ink on large sheets of white paper, briefly informing her of Raka's safe arrival and choosing to say nothing that might give away her resentment, her grievance.

As she folded the sheets and slipped them into a large envelope, she set her lips together and decided to make it clear to Raka – that Raka was a perceptive child was clear to *her* – that she was not part of Nanda Kaul's life, that she had her own place and might stay in it.

Seeing her emerge from the dark like a soundless moth, or dawdle up the path nursing a hand swollen and red with nettle stings, Nanda Kaul turned her head slightly and called to Ram Lal 'Is the child's bath water hot?' and Raka would slip past her on her way to her bath.

So they worked out the means by which they would live together and each felt she was doing her best at avoiding the

46

other but found it was not so simple to exist and yet appear not to exist.

Nanda Kaul could not help finding the child's long absences as perturbing as her presence was irksome. Occasionally she found herself walking restlessly from room to room or from one end of the garden to the other, not in search – it was not in her to search out another – but because the child's arrival and disappearance were so disquieting.

She was like a rabbit conjured up by a magician – drawn unwillingly out of the magic hat, flashing past Nanda Kaul, then vanishing in the dark of a bagful of tricks.

There was nothing nastier to Nanda Kaul's mind than magic.

Why should the calm of her existence be drawn taut, tense by speculation on this child's wanderings? So, when Raka did turn up, unpunctually, her legs scratched and the pockets of her dress stained with raspberry juice, Nanda Kaul turned a look on her that was reproachful rather than welcoming.

But Raka ignored her. She ignored her so calmly, so totally that it made Nanda Kaul breathless. She eyed the child with apprehension now, wondering at this total rejection, so natural, instinctive and effortless when compared with her own planned and wilful rejection of the child.

Seeing Raka bend her head to study a pine cone in her fist, the eyelids slipping down like two mauve shells and the short hair settled like a dusty cap about her scalp, Nanda Kaul saw that she was the finished, perfected model of what Nanda Kaul herself was merely a brave, flawed experiment.

It made her nostrils flare and her fingers twitch but she had to admit that Raka was not like any other child she had known, not like any of her own children or grandchildren. Amongst them, she appeared a freak by virtue of never making a demand. She appeared to have no needs. Like an insect burrowing through the sandy loam and pine-needles of the hillsides, like her own great-grandmother, Raka wanted only one thing – to be left alone and pursue her own secret life amongst the rocks and pines of Kasauli.

If Nanda Kaul was a recluse out of vengeance for a long life of duty and obligation, her great-granddaughter was a recluse by nature, by instinct. She had not arrived at this condition by a long route of rejection and sacrifice – she was born to it, simply.

Standing by the railing at the back of the house and watching the child carefully lower herself down the cliff to the kilns and agaves and refuse of the ravine, Nanda Kaul felt a small admiration for her rise and stir.

Chapter 5

Raka dropped lower and lower down the ravine. The lower she went the hotter it grew. Red dust settled between her toes and sandpapered her sandals. Runnels of sweat trickled from under her arms and behind her knees. The plain below opened wide its yellow mouth and it was its oven breath that billowed up the mountainside and enclosed her.

But she ignored that great hot plain below. Her eye was on the heart of the agaves, that central dagger guarded by a ring of curved spikes, on the contortions of the charred pine trunks and the paralysed attitudes of the rocks.

The refuse that the folds of the gorge held and slowly ate and digested was of interest too. There were splotches of blood, there were yellow stains oozing through paper, there were bones and the mealy ashes of bones. Tins of Tulip ham and Kissan jam. Broken china, burnt kettles, rubber tyres and bent wheels.

Once she came upon a great, thick yellow snake poured in rings upon itself, basking on the sunned top of a flat rock. She watched it for a long while, digging her toes into the slipping red soil, keeping still the long wand of broom she held in her hand. She had seen the tips of snakes' tails parting the cracks of rocks, she had seen slit eyes watching her from grottoes of shade, she had heard the slither of scales upon the ground, but she had never seen the whole creature before. Here was every part of it, loaded onto the stone, a bagful, a loose soft sackful of snake.

Leaving it to bask, she slid quietly on downwards, and now sweat ran from her face, too, trickled out between the roots of her hair in springs.

She shaded her eyes to look up at the swords of the Pasteur Institute chimneys piercing the white sky, lashed about with black whips of smoke. Raka sniffed the air and smelt cinders, smelt serum boiling, smelt chloroform and spirit, smelt the smell of dogs' brains boiled in vats, of guinea pigs' guts, of rabbits secreting fear in cages packed with coiled snakes, watched by doctors in white.

She licked her dry lips and tasted salted flakes of sweat. She dropped her eyes and gazed down at the plains, smothered in dust so that she could not make out cities, rivers or roads. Only the Chandigarh lake gleamed dully, metallically – a snake's eye, watching. Dust storms tore across the plain, rushing and lifting the yellow clouds higher and higher up the mountainside.

Raka began to scramble uphill. As she went, storming through soil and gravel, starting small avalanches of pebbles and loud, clanking ones of empty tins, she disturbed the crickets and made them raise their voices in alarm. Like a chorus singing and singing at the back of a stage, they sang in some difficult tongue she had not met before – not in Geneva, nor in New York, nor anywhere in that polyglot world she had once been led through. Was it Sanskrit? Was it Greek? It was complicated, shrill, incessant and Raka shook and shook her head to get the buzz out, half-closed her eyes against the glare and dust and had her thigh slashed by the blade of a fierce agave. Small beads of blood bubbled out of the white streak of the scratch. She doubled over to lick them, then hauled herself up over the lip of the cliff.

By a slight error in calculation, she came up not in the Carignano garden but into the backyard of the Kasauli club. She halted, stumbled a bit at this dismaying error, then saw that all the doors and windows of the green-roofed building were shut and there was no one about. She skirted the kitchen, allowing herself a glance out of the corner of her eye at its vast blackened oven, its acres of wooden tabletops, its cupboards of damp china and dull silver, all limp and lifeless at this hour. Ducking her head, she edged past the honeysuckle-hung porch, dashed across the garden where salvias and hydrangeas wilted, unwatered, and tumbled out onto the road that led up to Carignano.

Chapter 6

Ram Lal had stoked up the *hamam* with splinters of firewood and filled its round brass drum with water for Raka's bath. Having lit it, he sat down beside it on a flat stone outside the kitchen door, and smoked a quiet *biri*.

Then Raka came sliding down the knoll and almost on top of him – a bird fallen out of its nest, a nest fallen out of a tree – with grass sticking out of her hair and thorns stuck into her sandals. Sucking a finger that tended to get stuck in adventures, she sat down beside the *hamam*, listening to it thrum with heat like a steamboat. When the water was hot,

Ram Lal would spin the tap at the side, fill a brass bucket and carry it into her bathroom. The dust and grime would flow in a soapy sludge through the green drain hole into the lily bed outside. Till then, they would sit together.

'I saw a snake, Ram Lal,' she told him.

He took the *biri* out of his mouth. 'Here?'

'No, down in the ravine,' she said, pointing towards the cliff which was melting into an orange haze now that the sun was dropping westwards through the dustclouds over the plains.

'A cobra?'

'It was big – this big,' she said, showing him with her arm, 'And yellow. It was sleeping.'

'Yellow? This big? Ah,' said Ram Lal, settling his *biri* back between his lips. 'That was a *daman*. A rat snake. A good snake to have around.'

'It was quite far down, really.'

'Don't go that far,' Ram Lal said sharply. 'I told you not to – it isn't good.'

'I wanted to see a jackal. I've never seen a jackal. I hear them at night.'

'Why do you want to see a jackal? Didn't I tell you, they are mad? If they bite you, you will have to go to the Pasteur Institute and get fourteen injections – in the stomach. I did once.'

'Do jackals bite?'

'Of course. Jackals are as fierce as cobras. That place there,' he waved into the dust in which the forms of the pine trees were only barely visible now, writhing in the wind, 'is very bad, not safe. Why don't you go to the club and play with the *babas* there?'

'I did go. But there were no *babas* there. No one.'

'You should go in the evening, at the proper time,' he said primly, suddenly recalling better days, spent in service of richer, better homes. 'You should have an ayah. Then she

51

could wash you and dress you in clean clothes at four o'clock and take you down to the club. You would meet nice *babas* there. They come in the evenings with their ayahs. They play on the swings and their parents play bridge and tennis. Then they have lemonade and Vimto in the garden. That is what you should do,' he told her, severely.

Raka listened to him create this bright picture of hill-station club life politely rather than curiously. It was a life she had observed from the outside – in Delhi, in Manila, in Madrid – but had never tried to enter. She had always seemed to lack the ticket. 'Hmm,' she said, picking at a nicely crusty scab on her elbow.

'Don't do that,' Ram Lal said sharply, still speaking out of that proper and ordered world in the distance to which he had once belonged. 'You will make it bleed again and it will leave an ugly scar. You get so dirty crawling about on the hillsides.'

'I will soon bathe,' Raka assured him, and shifted on her bottom with impatience at this new censoriousness of his.

'Yes, I had better take your bucket in before the dust-storm arrives. Look, look, it is coming,' he shouted, holding down his cap about his ears as the wind tore across.

Raka stood up on the stone to watch the dense yellow haze gather and hurl itself across the plains, blotting out the scattered villages and mango groves, sweep on to the foot of the mountain and then, as if in rage at finding its way blocked, mounting the hillside, lifting higher and higher till it swept over the cliff and engulfed Kasauli, blotting out the view, the sky and the air in a gritty mass.

Ram Lal caught her by the shoulder and pushed her into the kitchen, shutting the door behind them. She went immediately to the window, wiped off the grime and peered out.

A white hen was lifted into the air and tossed past the

window in a frantic, fluttery arc, its squawks snatched out of its beak and shattered like glass.

The sun was bobbing in and out of the dust clouds, lighting them up in a great conflagration – a splendid bonfire that burned in the heart of the yellow clouds. The whole world was livid, inflamed. Only the closest pine trees showed, black silhouettes lashing from side to side.

'The *hamam* will be knocked over!' Ram Lal yelled. 'All that boiling water and fire!'

'Will it set fire to the garden?' shouted Raka. 'Will it set the hill on fire?'

'Don't know, don't know,' he muttered worriedly, grinding the palms of his hands together. 'This is how forest fires do start. I can't tell you how many forest fires we see each year in Kasauli. Some have come up as far as our railing. You can see how many of the trees are burnt, and houses too. Once the house down the hill, South View, was burnt down to the ground before the fire engine arrived.'

'Could they drive it down the hill to South View?'

'Yes, they dragged it down by jeeps, but there was no water. There is a water shortage every summer in Kasauli. There was no water to put out the fire and the whole house burnt down, and the cowshed with two buffaloes in it.'

'I've seen a burnt hut up on top of that hill there, on the upper Mall,' Raka remembered.

'Hut? It was a beautiful cottage. An English Mem lived there. It was burnt down in a forest fire and she went mad and was taken to the lunatic asylum with her arms and legs tied with rope. They say all her hair was burnt off, even her eyelashes, when she went in to save her cat. The watchman says he can still hear the cat howling in the ruins at night.'

'Can he? Can you? Have you? At midnight?'

But Ram Lal was too worried about his *hamam* of boiling water to tell her ghost stories now. He came to the window and stared out, trying to make out its brass shape in the

53

broiling dust. They could hear the grit and gravel flying and dashing against the stone walls and tin roofs, raucous poltergeists of the storm.

'If it falls over, all that dry grass will be set on fire,' he worried. 'And I'm old,' he groaned suddenly, sticking one finger in an ear and giving his head a shake. 'I can't run to the fire brigade. I can't run to fetch water. My knees hurt.'

'I'll do it,' Raka cried. 'I can run, Ram Lal – fast, fast.'

But the dust was subsiding, so was the roar of the wind. They could hear each other without shouting. The dense mass parted and thinned, began to tuck and tidy itself away like a tantrum that was spent. The air was pale, subdued.

Ram Lal opened the door and hurried over to his *hamam*. Raka followed.

The still air was cool now, edged with chill. The heat of the sun was gone like an angry crab put to flight, leaving its dull white shell behind – stranded, harmless.

The hills were chastened and austere in the chilly light.

Dizzy parrots, in a phosphorescent flock, burst out of the pines and spurted away, leaving their shrieks behind.

Ram Lal patted the solid flanks of the old *hamam*. 'A good thing we brought this up to Kasauli with us,' he said proudly. 'You don't get solid brass like this any more. Come along, the water's just right for your bath and I must go and sweep up all the dust in the house,' and he spun the little tap, gay with relief, filled a big bucket and carried it across the backyard to the green backdoor of her bathroom, Raka skipping behind him like a pet insect.

Striking an identical note of gay relief, a cuckoo called on the knoll.

Nanda Kaul, standing behind a closed window, watched them cross the yard – Ram Lal with the brass bucket from which bright drops spilt and flew as he lurched under its weight, Raka's spindly legs snapping at his heels like a pair of scissors.

54

Her hand shot out of the folds of silk and slapped at a pair of bumbling flies on the pane. They fell together on the windowsill, buzzing in alarm.

Chapter 7

Carefully returning her tea-cup to the tray, Raka rose and made a furtive sideways movement that always preceded her liquid, unobtrusive slipping away.

Very quickly Nanda Kaul, too, put down her cup and made a bustling movement with her knees that shook the table-top and made things rattle.

'I think I'll come with you today,' she said, very precisely, with an authoritative lift of her chin. 'For a walk.'

Raka stood still, dismayed. It was quite clear she was dismayed. Nanda Kaul saw that she did not care for her company. What she did not know was that the child always rose hungry from the tea-table and that her evening rambles about the hills were also forages for food, that she searched for berries and pine nuts along the paths to allay the hunger that grew and growled inside her small flat belly. She was never able to eat enough at a meal to last her till the next. Nor could she bear to ask for a biscuit. So she went hungry till dinner, unless she found a bush with ripe berries still popping out of its thorns or a bunch of sour oxalis leaves to chew.

Held back by her great-grandmother's sudden, unwelcome whim, she stood swaying on the top step of the veranda and looked uncertain.

'Wait a minute,' said Nanda Kaul briskly. 'I'll change into my walking shoes.'

Raka sighed and slipped down on the step beside a pot of fuchsias and swung the purple tasselled bells with her finger, despondently. Listening to her great-grandmother moving about in the bedroom, she felt as if she heard the sounds of collar and chain. She had not a dog's slavishness to companionship, and bit her lip with vexation.

It occurred to her that the old lady's idea of a walk might be a stroll through the bazaar amongst the holiday crowds, or down to the club for a lemonade and a chat with summer visitors around a table in the garden, and she grew more apprehensive.

But Nanda Kaul appeared in cracked grey gym shoes and a hefty walking-stick in her hand. 'Shall we go all the way to Monkey Point today?' she asked pleasantly, slightly swinging the stick.

They had never walked together before and made an awkward pair, now bumping into each other and politely apologizing, then wandering so far apart that they no longer seemed to belong to each other. Both walked stiffly, held themselves very upright, not letting themselves go with a natural stride.

It was a subdued afternoon, the hills sere, slashed everywhere by the charred trunks of burnt pines, jagged by the shapes of tumbled rocks and static boulders. The sun and summer dust fused into a dull mealy mass in which no light quickened but for the glisten of pine-needles when the wind ruffled them.

Now and then Nanda Kaul paused, her face rather pinched and her breathing quick, but it was not to catch her breath, she made clear, only to lift her stick and point out something of interest to Raka.

'Look, from here you have a perfect view of the plains on a clear day. If it weren't for the dust, you could see all the way to Ambala.

'Up on the hill there, Raka, you will see the burnt black

shell of a house. It was burnt down in a terrible forest fire one summer when there wasn't a drop of water to fight it with. An old lady lived there alone and they say she went mad and was put away. Poor woman, I wonder if she would not have preferred to die in the fire.' The walking-stick tapped the pebbles about her feet before she lifted it and waved it again. 'It looks dreadful, as if it is about to fall apart, but one shower of rain will bring out hundreds of flowers – lilies, dahlias – that she must have planted. You'll see them one day.

'D'you see that pleasant cottage there? The doctors of the Pasteur Institute have taken it over, several of them. A pity, it used to be so beautifully kept at one time, and look at it now. It still has a tennis court but it's used as a chicken run now. And the Garden House across the road – you can scarcely believe it now, but it once had the most beautiful garden in Kasauli. Now used as an army billet. The army's everywhere.

'I see they're up that hill, too. What is that peculiar instrument on top? Frightening. Like an atomic reactor. Or some such scientific monstrosity. And so much barbed wire around. A shame.'

They walked silently along the sere, silent hillsides on which boulders seemed to have been arrested in downward motion, precariously, and nothing grew on the pine-needle-spread earth but a few tangles of wild raspberries, hairy with thorn, and giant agaves in curious contorted shapes. Tourists and passers-by often scratched their names into the succulent blades and there they remained – names and dates, incongruous and obtrusive as the barbed wire.

'Too many tourists. Too much army. How they are ruining this – this quiet place,' Nanda Kaul said bitterly, her breath coming faster and her step fumbling. 'It really is – is saddening. One would have liked to keep it as it was, a – a haven, you know. When I first came here, I used to think of

Gerard Manley Hopkins' poem – do you know it? I used to be reminded of it constantly:

> 'I have desired to go
> Where springs not fail,
> To fields where flies no sharp and sided hail
> And a few lilies blow.

> 'And I have asked to be
> Where no storms come,
> Where the green swell is in the havens dumb,
> And out of the swing of the sea.'

'Of course it was not written about a place, any place, but about a vocation – a nun's vocation, as it happens – but, all the same, it seemed to apply.'

Her voice strengthened on this last line, grew brisk and lightened. Suddenly she laughed aloud. 'Look, Raka,' she cried, and did not need to point with her stick for the turbulence in a grove of chestnut trees was suddenly and vividly visible and audible. The swinging and leaping of branches, the crashing through leaves and showering of horse chestnuts showed clearly enough the source of her amusement – a wild horde of black-faced *langurs*, those fierce, lithe panthers of the monkey world, more feline than simian. Raka, too, threw her head back on her shoulders and laughed with her great-grandmother at the face an old *langur* made at them from the top of the tree, baring its teeth and gibbering, then jumping up and down on its bottom in anger and derision. Both admired with swift-flowing extravagance the still, silvery calm of a mother *langur* that sat stretching its long legs out along a branch and cradling an infant with a crumpled face in its elegant arm. The infant looked strangely aged, as if by worries and anxieties beyond its age, its little face black and wrinkled, its tear-drop eyes glistening with sadness. Others were clowns and bounced

58

and swung with boastful grace, playing Tarzan in the trees. Clapping their hands to their mouths, they hallooed like cinema heroes of the wilds, then leapt all in a bunch onto the tin roof of a half-ruined house with such a bang and a bombardment that children ran out of the house and servants from the kitchen, all shouting, all shooing till the herd took to its heels and vanished over the lip of the hill.

Raka and Nanda Kaul went downhill, laughing, at a quicker pace – refreshed.

'That old house is used as a summer holiday home for Delhi schoolchildren, you know,' Raka was sorry to hear her great-grandmother resume the guided tour patter. 'You wouldn't think it a safe place for children, would you? There are hardly any windowpanes left and the wood's rotten. But they do seem to have a happy time, I must say. I see them going for walks and picnics, even to church on Sundays, with their Indian Christian matron.

'Would you like to go to school in Kasauli, Raka? Perhaps as a boarder at Sanawar?'

Raka was so shocked, she could only shake her head dumbly, hating this craftiness, rejecting outright the very thought of school, of hostels, of discipline, order and obedience.

Quickening her pace, she outstripped Nanda Kaul and went downhill at a run, looking down at her toes pushed beyond the scuffed lip of her sandals, pressing into the dust and the dry pine-needles, painfully.

At the bottom of the hill, she stopped and waited for her great-grandmother to catch up which she did in a little while – panting, dusty and not a little ruffled by the child's abrupt and total rejection of what had been an invitation – a unique invitation, did she only know it – to stay on in these hills, with Nanda Kaul, and make them her home.

Chapter 8

They had come to a small grove of old, twisted, flowerless crêpe myrtles at the foot of Monkey Point. The municipal corporation had built some benches and some concrete shelters, like bus-stands, under the trees. It had the shabby, desolate air of a deserted bus-stop. Nevertheless, Nanda Kaul sank down onto one of the benches. Above them rose the jagged peak of Monkey Point, very high above them in the lucid radiance of the evening sky.

'I really don't think I can manage that climb, Raka,' she said, and her voice trembled a little with fatigue. 'If you feel like it, do go up on your own and I'll wait for you and watch.'

So she sat, resting, and watched with both alarm and admiration as Raka went hurtling away, grabbing at rocks and tufts of bleached grass, scrambling up the almost sheer face of the hill, doubled up with her knees often just under her chin, then stretched out as far as they would go, then suddenly popping up onto a higher ledge. Unseeing, she almost ran into a goat, then a kid, then a whole herd that came springing down, leapt over her back and flew like birds, landing at Nanda Kaul's feet and tripping nimbly homewards, the small goatsherd casually whistling and sauntering after them.

In no time at all, it seemed, the child had reached the top of the hill and stood bracing herself against the wind as it tried to lift her and blow her away.

She had not wanted to come here with her great-grandmother. She had planned to come to Monkey Point alone, on a solitary afternoon expedition, without anyone's knowing. Secrecy was to have been the essence of it, she relished it so – Raka had all the jealous, guarded instincts of an explorer, a discoverer, she hated her great-grandmother intently watching her ascent, clenching her hands with tension when the goats nearly knocked her off her feet or when she slipped on the loose pebbles. As she scrambled up, her resentment at the mention of boarding-school at Sanawar was still inside her chest, tight as a stone. But now it blew away with the wind, leaving her light and exhilarated, airborne as a seed or a blade of grass.

The wind swung her about and threatened to throw her onto her knees. But she held her hair down about her ears and held onto a rock with her toes, hearing it whip at her dress, and was sure that if she let go, if she spread out her arms and rose on her toes, she would fly, fly off the hill-top and down, down on currents of air, like the eagles that circled slowly, regally below her.

She was higher than the eagles, higher than Kasauli and Sanawar and all the other hills: they were as low and soft as banks of golden moss far below. To the south the plain stretched endlessly out and away, no longer hot and livid under the summer sun but calm and still and cat-grey in the dusk, raked by the shining flow of Punjab's five rivers and Chandigarh's lake set in its breast like a dull silver brooch – not set so much as floating a little above the flatness, suspended in the dusk. There was a breadth of space, a vast, sweeping depth to the scene. Raka thought it like an ancient scroll unrolled at her feet for her to survey.

To the north, the soft, downy hills flowed, wave upon wave, gold and blue and violet and indigo, like the sea. The sound of the wind rushing up through the pines and then receding was the sound of the sea.

I'm shipwrecked, Raka exulted, I'm shipwrecked and

61

alone. She clung to a rock – my boat, alone in my boat on the sea, she sang.

So she stood, rocking, her feet placed wide-apart, her ear-drums thrumming with the roar of the waves and the wind, till she began to get an ear-ache, grew aware of the darkness gathering, remembered the old lady waiting on the bench below, and began to make her way reluctantly downhill, finding it simplest just to sit down and slide roughly down on her bottom.

It was quite dark at the foot of the hill, in the crêpe myrtle grove. The old lady rose to meet Raka in agitation. When she saw the child was whole, her bones intact, she made some scolding sounds in relief, and they walked home-wards in a great silence which was rent now and then by the clear, ringing call of some invisible bird that defied night.

When they reached Carignano the lights were on. The hills were black waves in the night, with the lights of the villages and towns so many lighted ships out at sea.

A nightjar began to cackle. Ram Lal came hurrying to open the gate for them.

'What's for dinner?' cried Raka, running forwards.

Chapter 9

The walk to Monkey Point had not been a success after all for Nanda Kaul did not suggest another. Over tea, she would open a book and read – she had three or four on a table at her side, always: Gogol's *Dead Souls*, Waley's trans-lation of Chinese poems, a book on Indian birds by Salim Ali – and when Raka rose and furtively slipped off the veranda by herself, she would turn a leaf and frown with greater concentration.

As soon as Raka was out of sight, however, she would put down her book and hurry up the knoll from where she could survey a great length of the Upper Mall as it snaked around the hills. Here ladies and gentlemen on holiday perambulated sedately and their children took turns at riding Kasauli's two ponies, Rani and Rolo, almost equally sedately.

But Raka rarely walked on the Mall, Upper or Lower. As soon as she could do so without being seen, she slipped under the railing that kept pedestrians and horses from plunging off the road and down the precipice, and disappeared down the paths that were barely marked on the crisp grass and pine-needles and that only goats and villagers ever used. Keeping to these paths, she knew a Kasauli that neither summer visitors nor upright citizens of the town ever knew. She did not shirk the rubbish chutes or the servants' latrines constructed of tin amongst the nettles. She visited villages down in the valleys and saw the wheat being threshed by mechanically treading cattle, and corn and pumpkins being dried on rooftops. The village women and children glanced at her but never spoke. Once she saw the red fur of a fox momentarily lit by a trick of sunlight before it disappeared between immense rocks. Once she heard a shot and then saw a boy saunter past with a gun over his shoulder and a pheasant dangling from his hand. She averted her eyes from him and plunged off the path into the raspberries and broom. Mostly she saw no one. She had the gift of avoiding what she regarded as dispensable.

Sensing this, Nanda Kaul was perturbed. She could not tell why she wanted to bring Raka out into the open. It was not how she herself chose to live. She did not really wish to impose herself, or her ways, on Raka. Yet she could not leave her alone.

Raka's genius. Raka's daemon. It disturbed.

At tea, she asked Raka, 'Why don't you go down to the club sometimes?'

Raka was as alarmed by this as by the suggestion that she go to boarding-school at Sanawar.

'Didn't your mother and father take you to clubs, to parties?' Nanda Kaul probed, uncharacteristically, and her very nose seemed to stretch longer as she leaned forward.

Raka shook her head, untruthfully. Her father had made attempts, sporadically, 'to bring her out of her shell' as he called it, by taking her to tea at a restaurant and insisting, in Madrid, that her mother invite children to tea on her birthday. These had been painful occasions – as painful for Raka as for her broken, twittering mother. They had not been repeated. Her long illness in Delhi and her weak, exhausted state thereafter had absolved her of any further need to 'socialize'. It had seemed months that she had been in bed, her hair shorn down to the scalp, feeling the stale air stirred by the revolving blades of the electric fan, her eyes shut while her mother read to her in a sepulchral voice that never changed its pitch and never disturbed her out of her deep, secret thoughts. One might have thought she still moved about in a kind of dream, set to the sound of cicadas and the wind in the pines instead of her mother's martyred voice and the revolving electric fan.

Looking down at her foot where a mosquito had raised a small red bump on the little toe, Raka said in a stifled voice, 'But you never go to the club either, Nani.'

Nanda Kaul's foot gave an astonished little jerk inside the grey silk tent of her sari. Then she gave a snort of laughter. Bending down so that her face was at a level with the hunched child's and her nose tapered softly forwards, she said 'Raka, you really *are* a great-grandchild of mine, aren't you? You are more like me than *any* of my children or grandchildren. You are *exactly* like me, Raka.'

But Raka retreated pell-mell from this outspoken advance. It was too blatant, too obvious for her who loved secrecy above all. Her small face blanched and she pinched her lips together in distaste.

Nanda Kaul was equally shocked. Quickly straightening her back, she sat back in her chair, stiffly. By the manner in which she tensed herself and drew strict lines down her face and folded her hands in her lap stilly, it was clear she was trying to repair her authority, her composure, her distance in age.

They averted their faces from each other.

Nanda Kaul surveyed the woollen hills. Raka stared up at the hoopoe's nest in the eaves, concealed from sight and giving itself away only by the whirring and whistling of the nestlings whenever the mother arrived with a mouthful for them. They were silent except when she arrived and stirred them up into a clamour. She spent her day flying back and forth, catching insects for them, her beak snapping upon dragonflies and moths with sharp clicks. Till lately there had been ripe apricots at her doorstep and there was hardly an apricot Raka picked up from the grass that didn't bear the mark of her long beak. Raka had come out into the wet grass early in the mornings to eat apricots before breakfast and the hoopoe had watched jealously from the trees as she wandered about barefoot, looking for the sweetest and the ripest. But there were few left now that Ram Lal had cooked jam and stored it in great jars of honey-coloured conserve on the pantry shelves, and the hoopoe had had to make up the loss by catching moths in mid-air and dragging worms out of the earth. Sometimes the father bird helped. Sometimes they fought tremendous battles with the cocky little crested bul-buls, yellow-bibbed, yellow-bottomed and outrageously cheeky. Now that Raka and her great-grandmother were sitting on the veranda, looking for a way to break apart and move away, the hoopoes sat disconsolately in the apricot tree, looking baffled and distressed.

At last Raka burst out 'If we don't go away, they won't be able to feed their babies.'

'Who?' asked Nanda Kaul, looking around with suspicion.

'The hoopoes over there.'

'Oh,' said Nanda Kaul. 'I wondered who you meant. Babies – hmm,' her voice was disdainful. 'Well, run along, you'll be wanting your evening walk.'

Chapter 10

She did go to the club after all, found herself there to her own surprise. Not in the afternoon, with the little shrill girls from New Delhi in their frilly frocks and new shoes, not to have lemonade or watch, giggling, the billiard players in the back room, but in the dark of the night when the big party of the summer season was held.

Ram Lal had talked to her about it.

'Of course it is not like the old days any more,' he said, puffing at his *biri* beside the quiet *hamam*, 'when the Angrez Sahibs and Memsahibs had dances, but the army is something like them. They also have the band come from the cantonment for the evening, and drink whisky and dance.'

'How is it different then?' Raka asked, squatting on her heels beside him and tugging at a square of quartz embedded in the mosaic of less attractive pebbles in the ground. She continued the conversation only because Ram Lal had nothing more interesting to say that evening.

'They used to roast whole sheep over a spit,' Ram Lal said, widening his rheumy eyes so that they flared red.

'Whole sheep. And hundreds of bottles of spirits were drunk, hundreds.'

'And now?'

'Now,' Ram Lal contemptuously spat out, 'now it is nothing like that.' But he could not say in what way times had fallen, how they had worsened or lessened. He really had no intercourse with the club cooks and too little information. He could only indicate it by scornful gestures and the spitting out of shreds of tobacco.

So, when at night she heard the band strike up on the other side of the knoll, curiosity made her put on a sweater over her pyjamas and climb out of the window. She tumbled quietly out into the darkness, very thick in Kasauli where lights were few and widely separated, and silent now that the breeze had dropped, except for the grieving wails of the jackals down in the ravine and the equally lugubrious hammer and howl of the band at which the nightjars laughed, harshly and raucously, out of the trees and bushes of the night.

It was too dark to see but Raka could feel her way up the knoll at speed and then she slid down the hillside almost onto the kitchen roof that thrummed and bellowed with noise, activity and the heat from many fires and many ill-tempered cooks.

Her feet were too small and light to crunch the pebbly gravel, they only seemed to brush over it as she went quietly round by the back of the club house, past the row of green bathroom doors, all shut and emanating green damp, to the billiard room which was lit and where some tentatively whiskery boys were knocking around balls on the green lawn of the table. The windows were uncurtained, the light from the china-shaded bulb fell on the dark gravel in sheets of white paper and made Raka afraid of being seen by these newly hairy young men with their long awkward limbs that seemed unsynchronized and unhinged by youth so that

67

there was something more alarming about them, to her, than in the wails of the jackals or the sudden rattles of the nightjars in the darkness.

How much friendlier she found darkness. She sidled past the lighted windows into a tunnel of dark between the club wall and the hillside. Ferns brushed against her. A clutter of hoes, spades and gardeners' baskets tripped her. Then she was at the corner and saw she would have to cross the garden if she were to reach the ballroom at the other end of the building. For a minute she contemplated retreat, then she remembered what Ram Lal had told her about fancy dress balls, how ladies dressed as queens and men as princes, and drank sparkling spirits that made them sing. So she made a quick, convulsive dash, lowering her head and refusing to see people coming and going, always in groups and clusters, all laughing, and no one looked at her, it was as if the lumpy grey sweater she had pulled over her head had made her invisible.

Now she was in the veranda outside the ballroom and she slid in between pots of geraniums and the empty wine-racks that were used to stack up a wall, and burrowed into a dusty hole amongst the pieces of chalk and an old blackboard with bingo numbers marked up on it. She parted the thick green curtains and applied her nose to the parting, breathed in its mildewed dust, shut one eye and focused the other on the illuminated scene of cantonment revelry inside.

Chapter 11

Then she fell on her knees with shock.

This was not what Ram Lal had led her to expect. This was no vision of kings and queens in a rosy court.

To the heated drumming of the band, madmen and rioters leapt, bowed, swayed and jigged, costumes flying, paper horns blowing. It was lunacy rampant. Raka held her head between her hands, she thought it would crack in two.

She wished she could close her eyes. She wished she were a million miles away from the band. She tried to think she was asleep and this was a nightmare.

But a man in green leapt out from almost under her nose and shot up at the ceiling, his feet in green socks flapping. He should have fiddled like a grasshopper but he crowed like a cock – or was that the trumpet?

A woman with a bucket on her head laughed inside it so that it was like a cooking spoon rattling in an empty pot. A figure in black answered her call and sidled up and bowed. When he straightened, Raka saw the skull and crossbones in white upon his chest. He had a scythe tucked under his arm and it glinted and shot off bolts of lights when he raised it and chopped off the woman's bucket head. Under her dishevelled hair her pink throat opened wide and she laughed in bubbles of blood. The bucket clanked across the floor and came to rest at Raka's foot. Her toes shrivelled.

An outsized monkey with a stiff, curling tail scampered over and kicked the bucket away, then turned a somersault and the band yipped and yayed and a man in rusty black and yellowed white sang:

> 'O take me out to the ball game,
> Take me out to the fair . . .'

Bunches of balloons sighed and swayed to the music, then suddenly shot up and squeaked with alarm as a lady mouse ran out from under them, her whiskers trembling like antennae and a long tail losing handfuls of fur across the floor. She was being chased by a man who had his hair combed down over his eyes and wore a scarf around his neck like a noose before it is tightened. He caught her by the tail, she jumped into his arms, they threw up their knees, laughed and turned. Two balloons exploded, bang-bang, without being pricked. Their shreds lay in a corner like rubber tears.

Rolling across to the chink where Raka's eye hid, a brown animal with a brush-tail spiked and bristling and eyes glaring like two black marbles with white snakes coiled inside them, cried 'Yip-yip-yip,' then 'Yip-yip-yippee', and stood up and drank a mug of beer. White specks stuck to the corner of its mouth and solidified there.

Into the midst of this rabble stalked a very tall man in white, a stethoscope about his neck and pink rubber gloves on his hands – very pink, too pink. Raka stiffened – for he lifted his pink rubber hands into the air and she thought he would now silence them all, stretch them out on the ball-room floor and perform the operation that would wash them all away in a river of blood.

Instead, the band took his gesture as a kind of signal, changed its tune, and the singer began to warble:

'You are my sunshine,
My only sunshine,
You make me ha-pee . . .'

and the doctor lowered his hands to the waist of a silver fish dressed in hundreds and hundreds of soda bottle tops, and they swung away together in a dance that made the fish's tail jingle and clank like a thousand broken bottles.

A walking maypole revolved slowly to the music, her pink and blue and yellow streamers twining and untwining about the green stalk of her body.

In walked a brass cage, a fat head for a bird, held in place with plastic clothes-peg claws. Arm in arm with the caged head-bird came a Pierrot in black and white and scarlet lipstick who suddenly ripped off his mask, revealing eyes as pink as a pig's flung it up into the air and began to prance, singing

70

> 'Mama, she loves Papa,
> Papa, he loves Mama . . .'

which made everyone laugh without ceasing and swing their bottoms from side to side, big and thick and heavy bottoms, all turned to face Raka's transfixed eye in the curtains.

Then the row of bottoms parted to let through a figure in a brown robe that came stalking straight up to Raka as though it saw her there behind the curtains. Yet it could not see for it had no head, only a shawl dipped in blood dripping about its neck. It held its head tucked underneath its arm, grinning like a pot, with too many teeth.

A whimper burst from Raka then, like a whimper from a pod or a bud when it is pricked, or pressed, and bursts. Shooting out of the corner like a seed from the burst pod, she threw down the blackboard, crushed the chalks underfoot, thrust past the stacked wine-racks and fled like an animal chased, sobbing '*Hate* them – *hate* them . . .' as she ran, her sweating fists beating her sides and her feet tearing through thorns, ferns and gravel. All the caged, clawed, tailed, headless male and female monsters followed her, pell-mell, prancing to the tune of The Bridge on the River Kwai:

> 'Ta-ra, ta-ra, ta-ra-ra
> Ta-ra . . .'

Somewhere behind them, behind it all, was her father, home from a party, stumbling and crashing through the curtains of night, his mouth opening to let out a flood of rotten stench, beating at her mother with hammers and fists of abuse – harsh, filthy abuse that made Raka cower under her bedclothes and wet the mattress in fright, feeling the stream of urine warm and weakening between her legs like a stream of blood, and her mother lay down on the floor and

71

shut her eyes and wept. Under her feet, in the dark, Raka felt that flat, wet jelly of her mother's being squelching and quivering, so that she didn't know where to put her feet and wept as she tried to get free of it. Ahead of her, no longer on the ground but at some distance now, her mother was crying. Then it was a jackal crying.

Wildly, Raka veered. She had been about to go down the ravine. But that was where the jackal cried. Turning, she found the windowsill, scrabbled over it and fell into her room. Then there was no sound at all but of her heart leaping and plopping in a black well, drowning out the music from the band on the other side of the knoll.

Chapter 12

There was something flushed about her thin invalid face after that. Her eyes darkened, as if with a secret she would not divulge. She was no longer the insect, the grasshopper child. She grew as still as a twig.

Then the twig would move and show itself an insect still. She still went down into the ravine to wander. Watching her surreptitiously from her window, then from the railing, Nanda Kaul, who had sensed a change, saw her slide down a chute of rubble and red earth to one of those ominous brick kilns under the Pasteur Institute, keeping herself steady on the steep incline by holding onto two tufts of blond grass. What was she looking at? Nanda Kaul could not make out or imagine, she saw only the tension in the straddled legs and the white knuckles. A branch of a pine tree dipped. A vulture had moved its claws up a little, shrugged its massive shoulders, stretched out its rubber-hose neck and belched. The child started. Then walked backwards, away from the

72

tree. Turning around abruptly, she dropped on all fours and came scrambling up the hill so fast that Nanda Kaul had to hurry in order to vanish into the kitchen in time not to be seen.

But Raka did not come up over the lip of the cliff. She must have taken another route of escape: she knew many. When her great-grandmother ventured back to look for her, there was no one in the ravine but a herd of goats nibbling at the sparse thorns and nettles with rubber-lipped greed and nervous avarice. Up on the hill the Pasteur Institute flung writhing snakes of smoke into the sky. Nanda Kaul pursed her lips at the ugly sight – it did so spoil the view. And added to the heat of the summer afternoon. What did Raka see in it? Why did it fascinate the child?

Missing out the tea that was always so disappointingly liquid and no more, Raka came in through the gate only late in the evening, tossing a horse chestnut from one hand to the other and chanting under her breath, defiantly and inaudibly 'I don't care – I don't care – I don't care for *anything*!'

She stopped as soon as she saw her great-grandmother who was strolling up and down over the pebbles of her garden with a rather exaggerated nonchalance. She glanced at Raka's dusty hair and scratched knees but only said 'If it doesn't rain soon, these hydrangeas will die.'

Raka came to look. They both stood gazing at the bush of leathery flowers that were turning brown at the edges. Under it a cicada shrilled and whirred frenziedly.

It was still light, still warm, and they strolled together, hands behind their backs and fingers clenched. They heard the two ponies clatter past on the Lower Mall and watched them carry two small blonde children down to the Alasia Hotel.

'Wouldn't you like to go for a pony ride, Raka?' Nanda Kaul asked. 'You could take one down to Monkey Point.'

'No,' said Raka shortly. 'It's no fun: that man always comes along.'

'Oh, the pony man,' said Nanda Kaul. 'No, that wouldn't be fun.'

'Look,' said Raka suddenly, small seeds of spit hissing out from behind her teeth. 'Is that the moon? Is that the full moon?' She pointed to a copper glow that outlined the shoulder of a hill in the east, then bloomed rapidly into the evening sky, a livid radiance in that cinereous twilight.

'N-no,' mused Nanda Kaul uncertainly. 'The moon's not nearly full, not nearly.'

Then little pin-pricks of light went up in the black mass of the hill. They exploded here and there, ran up and down in lines, burnt clearly. As the sky darkened, the glow reddened.

'It's a forest fire,' Nanda Kaul breathed out at last. 'A big fire, it seems. Oh, there's always a forest fire at this time of year.'

But it was the first Raka had seen. Shivers ran through her, zigzag, leaving streams of sweat in their wake. Hugging herself with bone-thin arms, she stood on one leg, then the other, waiting. It was far away, across the valley, they could neither smell the burning pine trees nor hear the crackling and hissing. It was like a fire in a dream – silent, swift and threatening.

Seeing her dance from foot to foot, Nanda Kaul said 'If you want to go to the bathroom, run along, Raka.'

Raka shook her head, but in a little while turned and fled. Nanda Kaul followed slowly. While shutting the door behind her, she took another look at the fire, now spilling down the hillside in runnels of sparks, in streams of heat.

'I wonder if the fire brigade will be able to do anything about it,' she said, shaking her head, as Raka came into the room and stood at the window beside her.

'What if they can't? What will happen?'

'Oh, it will burn itself out in the night, I expect. It will reach a dry, rocky belt and stop. Or they might try to stop it by building counter-fires. They certainly won't have enough water to put it out. There isn't a drop of water to spare in the Simla Hills, in June.'

'What about houses? What if houses burn?'

Nanda Kaul thrust out her lower lip and dropped her eye-lids. 'Yes, they will burn. Whole villages may burn in a fire that big.'

Raka stood looking through the window at what looked like a display of fireworks in the distance. Its soundlessness was eerie.

'Lucky it is not closer than it is to Kasauli, or Sanawar. We've had fires right here, at the edge of the town.'

Raka nodded. 'I've seen trees, all burnt.'

At night she kept getting out of bed and coming barefoot into the drawing-room to look out of the window and see the fire spread.

Nanda Kaul lay on her back in bed and heard the bare feet slapping softly on the tiles with a sound like damp cloth. It kept her awake – the feet going back and forth, obsessed.

Raka was aware of her great-grandmother's wakefulness. She heard her deep, tired sighs, but she had grown used to ignoring her. She went back and back again to the window to see if the fire had come any closer to Carignano, to Kasauli.

Occasionally a great cloud of illuminated smoke rose into the air and burst. Lower down the hill were only pinpricks, fireflies of light, constantly moving, gathering, dispersing.

Holding her ear to the cold pane closely, she thought she heard the cries of animals and birds burning in that fire. But when she removed her ear from the pane, she heard only the crepitation of silence. Once, the soft hooting of an owl.

The disturbed sky, livid with firelight, kept her awake: it was too light. If she fell asleep, she felt the fire might creep

75

up and catch her unawares. It had the quality of a dream –
disaster, dream-spectres that follow one, trap one.

But she went back and forth so often that eventually she
tired and fell onto the sofa and was found there, asleep in her
nightie, by Ram Lal next morning.

She woke to find the hills blotted out by smoke and
summer haze. The fire was blotted out, too. The north wind
brought with it a cindery smell and a layer of ashes that it
deposited on Kasauli like a grey pelt. Raka went about
thoughtfully drawing lines in it with her finger.

Chapter 13

One would have thought Raka searched Ram Lal out. Certainly she neither followed nor waited for anyone else,
thought Nanda Kaul, sourly, as she watched from the veranda while Raka hung about the kitchen for Ram Lal to
finish his work there and come out to light the *hamam* for
her bath. She noticed how, every evening – briefly, to be
sure – the two would sit together by the *hamam* in the
coppery light of those June evenings. Sitting together on
their heels, watching the eagles soar and glide soundlessly in
the gorge and out over the plains, they talked dreamily.
Ram Lal could arouse Raka's interest and hold it as Nanda
Kaul could not. Interest her, but at the same time give her
reassurance of safety. Nanda Kaul knew that a child needed
to have the two elements combined, but she could not, or
would not, be bothered to try, while Ram Lal did it naturally and comfortably, for Raka. The low pitch of their
voices conveyed the comfort in these conversations that she
could not hear, only observe.

'I saw you go down there last night,' Ram Lal said, drawing at his *biri* through his fist. 'That was bad.'

'Why? The moon was shining, I could see so clearly.'

'But you could be seen too.'

'There was no one to see.'

Ram Lal shook his head, knowingly. 'The *churails* were there. They see you.'

'Who?'

'*Churails*. Didn't you know they lived in that gorge there? They always live amongst the dead. They live off their flesh. They feast on the corpses the Institute doctors throw down after they have cut up the mad dogs and boiled their brains. If at night you hear sudden sounds, like shots, it is the *churails* cracking bones.'

Raka's eyes grew black hoops around them. She put one hand on his knee and asked 'What are they like?'

'Very big. Bigger than any man. Dressed in black so they can't be seen in the dark. Only their red eyes glow like coals. And their feet are turned backwards. That is the surest way to tell a *churail* – its feet are turned backwards.'

'But how will I see their feet in the dark?'

Now Ram Lal's eyes grew great black hoops. 'Don't,' he said. 'Don't look down at their feet. If you see red eyes glowing in the dark, just turn and run. I know a woman who turned to stone because she saw a *churail*'s feet. She was walking down to Garkhal at twelve o'clock on a moonlit night, and met a *churail*. I can show you the stone at the side of the road if you come with me.'

'Will you? Will you?' Raka cried.

She was answered by a sudden clamour as if the *churails* had arrived in one swoop, black-bat females, to avenge themselves – whooping and whistling, tearing through the air and thundering across the roof: a band of *langurs* had arrived. Pierrots in black and white, clowns and bandits at once – bawdy, raucous and marauding. Suddenly every tree

77

was full of them – their whip tails and jewel eyes, their mask faces and spider arms, black and grey and silver. They swung from the branches of the pines to the apricots and from there to the roof and sprinted across the corrugated iron sheets. They ran nimble-footed along the railing, dived through windows and shot through doors. Even as Ram Lal and Raka ran into their midst, yelling and waving their arms, they tore leaves off the apricot trees in search of fruit, plucked hydrangeas to bits, dashed into the kitchen and grabbed at potatoes, baring their teeth and gibbering at whoever came in the way. Robbers, bandits, they never forgot to be clowns and stun their spectators with acrobatics out of a jungle dream.

Then Ram Lal ran to the *hamam* and beat its side with a stick of kindling – tum-tum-tum-tum, it rang out a warning. Little herdsboys, those natural enemies of the *langurs*, swarmed up the hillside immediately, stones in their hands, panting to join the fray. 'Hroo, hroo, hroo,' they yelled till the *langurs* collected in a band and made off with giant leaps and swings, down the hillside and across the Mall into the valley. Only one portly mother was left behind, in the pine tree by the gate, her young one clinging to her belly with careful fingers, its face pinched and anxious. Ram Lal picked up a stone to hurl it at her but found Raka holding onto his arm with all her might, swinging from it like an anxious monkey herself.

'Leave her, leave her,' she begged.

'Hroo, hroo! Leave her to break our trees and steal our potatoes – what for?' growled Ram Lal but dropped the stone and, clapping his hands together, yelled 'Get off, you she-devil, you *churail*, you black-faced *hubshee*!' The *langur* bared her teeth at him, then groped her way down the tree-trunk with belly-rolling, bottom-swaying slowness specially to insult, climbed casually over the gate and loped away, the infant still clinging to her belly and peeping round it with bead-bright eyes.

78

There was a sudden stone-like stillness following the clamour of their arrival and dispersal. Nanda Kaul rose to her feet on the veranda and said coldly 'Ram Lal, you might clear those herdsboys off our garden now.'

What had pained her most was seeing Raka run after Ram Lal and swing from his arm. She had not even called to her Nani to come and see the *langurs*.

Chapter 14

When a letter came to inform them that Raka's mother Tara had had another breakdown and was in a nursing-home in Geneva and that Raka's grandmother Asha, having seen another grandchild safely into the world, was flying to Switzerland to be with her, Nanda Kaul pursed her lips, folded up the blue sheets of paper with that distasteful sprawl across them, and hid them in her desk.

If Raka had secrets from her, she intended to have secrets from her, too.

But it gave her an increased sense of Raka's dependence on her, Nanda Kaul. She was not sure if it was poignant, ironical or merely irritating that Raka herself remained totally unaware of her dependence, was indeed as independent and solitary as ever. Watching her wandering amongst the rocks and agaves of the ravine, tossing a horse chestnut rhythmically from hand to hand, Nanda Kaul wondered if she at all realized how solitary she was. She certainly never asked nor bothered to see if there were a letter for her, or news. Solitude never disturbed her. She was the only child Nanda Kaul had ever known who preferred to stand apart and go off and disappear to being loved, cared for and made the centre of attention. The children Nanda Kaul had known had wanted only to be such centres: Raka alone did not.

She even saw herself to bed each night, as no other child she knew had done, silently, and slept alone. Nanda Kaul would sit up in her chair, very stiffly, turning the pages of her book – at present *The Travels of Marco Polo* – and pretending not to see when the child got up and went out and down the passage to her room. Habit would rear its head inside her, make her prepare to follow, tell her to tuck the child in, read her a story and lead her safely into sleep. But she did not go – she sank back and sat still. She would not go. She had not come to Carignano to enslave herself again. She had come to Carignano to be alone. Stubbornly, to be alone.

Then she lay awake in her bed herself. It was not the demented jackals howling in the ravine that kept her awake. Nor the sudden clatter of pine cones on the roof or the soft hooting of the owls. It was the thought of Raka in the next room, here in her house.

She had not been asked to Carignano. Yet here she was, fitted in quietly and unobtrusively as an uninvited mouse or cricket.

Would she own it herself one day, Carignano? Nanda Kaul wondered, lashing her fingers together over her chest. Ought she to leave it to Raka? Certainly it belonged to no one else, had no meaning for anyone else. Raka alone understood Carignano, knew what Carignano stood for – she alone valued that, Nanda Kaul knew.

She thought of making a will. The thought was distasteful. It meant asking the lawyer over and she wished no one to come.

She wished no one to go either – certainly not Raka.

Chapter 15

A high wind whined through the pine trees all afternoon, lashing the branches and scattering the cones. Up on the knoll, Raka sat hugging her knees, watching the long-tailed rose-ringed parakeets that clung to the cones, biting out their sweet nuts, letting go with frantic shrieks as the wind knocked into them and tore away the cones, tossing them down the hill. Small white butterflies were being blown about like scraps of paper over the bleached grass, but the pairs would not be separated, they always found each other again and fluttered together, two by two.

When Nanda Kaul came out into the garden after her afternoon nap, to call Raka to tea, the greyness along the horizon had curdled into white and grey lumps that the wind was driving lower and lower across the Simla Hills. They stood together, watching.

'It's a storm from the north. How strange, at this time of year. We have dust-storms from the south, in June, and the monsoon follows them. We get north winds later in the year usually,' the old lady mused. The wind was whipping at her sari and cracking the silk folds against each other so she retreated to the veranda.

Over their tea they watched the clouds drop from the sky, swollen and heavy with cold, like a great polar bear crouching, hurrying over the hill-tops, its white fur settling on rooftops, brushing the hillsides, enclosing the pines. Then it was upon them. With it, the rain.

What rain! The house shook, the roof crackled, long raindrops slanted in. They rose, picked up the tea-tray and retreated to the drawing-room. It was dark here. A light was lit. The room took on the appearance of a shelter, warm, glowing. The downpour drummed on the taut tin roof, deafening. The coolness and wetness of the air refreshed, exhilarated – it was iced wine dashed in the face.

Raka could not sit still. She went to the window to watch, rubbing the pane with her nose. Or wandered about the room, touching things. She normally touched nothing in the house.

Nanda Kaul poured out another and another cup of tea, recklessly. She, too, felt a kind of restlessness, a release.

'We could be shipwrecked,' she said with a smile so unaccustomed that it was stiff and cracked. 'Water, water everywhere. What a storm.'

The wind flung the rain at the windowpane. Raka backed away, came and sat on a stool, put out a finger and stroked a little bronze Buddha that sat inscrutably smiling and stilly counting its beads on the tabletop.

Nanda Kaul looked down at the scratched brown finger with a dirty nail stroking the smooth bronze head. 'Isn't it a beautiful piece?' she said suddenly in a high, musical voice that did not sound as if it belonged to her. 'It comes all the way from Tibet, you know. My father brought it.'

Raka, her chin cupped in her hand, looked at the old lady in some surprise. No one had told her of her great-great-grandfather, or anyone else, ever having visited Tibet. But perhaps they had, and she had not listened. She was very selective about her listening. Now she did.

'That was long, long ago at a time when hardly anyone had even thought of trying to go to Tibet. Only the government could arrange such an expedition, and then it was with a great deal of military aid. Traders went, of course, for the sake largely of musk, that precious scent that is so highly prized all over the world. They would bring back other things, too – turquoise, gold and silver, carved idols and

82

brocades. But my father did not go either as an official or a trader. He went as an explorer, out of curiosity.' She rubbed the tips of her long, fine fingers together, nervously, as she talked, and gazed, not at Raka, but at the small, quiet Buddha. 'We had spent the summer in Kashmir, of course. At the end of it, in early autumn, he took us all with him as far as the Zoji-La Pass. It was a time when the orchards were all in their autumn colours – scarlet, crimson and rust. Leaving them below, and the little villages with their carved wooden houses, we went up into the forests of walnuts and maples, sycamores and chestnuts. Then through the pine and birch belt to the bare rocks and ice above. It seemed we were travelling in paradise with him. But one morning, when we had camped beside a river of green ice water in a meadow that seemed untouched by a single footprint, and the sky seemed the purest, cleanest sky there's ever been, he got onto his horse, Suleiman, dressed in fur and leather, and rode away over the pass, leaving us behind.' Her voice dropped to a murmur that Raka had to strain to overhear. It seemed to have died away altogether for the only sound was of rain, dashing against the windowpane and drumming on the roof.

Then her voice joined in the rain, in the rush. 'He wore leather boots up to his knees as he rode away, and the two flaps of his fur caps showed like ears, for a long way. His dog, a black Bhotiya we called Demon, followed him. They all splashed through the icy river and disappeared on the rocks. We returned to Srinagar.

'He was away in Tibet – oh, for years, years. He went every step of the way on horseback, or on foot. The Mustagh Pass, the Baltoro glacier, the Aghil Pass . . . a terribly hard, dangerous route.'

As the rain softened, her voice rose, unnaturally. 'He travelled all over Tibet, had the strangest experiences. He spent nights in tiger-infested bamboo forests where the people used to burn green bamboos that would burst at the joints with such loud explosions as to frighten off wild animals for miles. He joined in their famous archery competitions – you know, there are legendary archers in Tibet who can shoot arrows for longer distances than anyone believes possible. He went hunting with them, sometimes with falcons and sometimes with packs of dogs that were as large as asses, for musk deer whose musk is sold to traders for silver. Can you believe it, agents come all the way from Paris in search of musk for their perfumeries, and have bought as much as a million ounces of silver worth at a time.

'He saw them dredge gold from their rivers and salt from their salt springs. This is dried and shaped into cakes that are almost as precious as gold. In fact, forty or sixty cakes of salt could buy a saggio of gold. Then they love jewellery there – turquoise and coral, silver and gold. The women are loaded with them as the men with furs – ermine and sable.

'In certain areas there were clove trees – rather like laurel, he said – and ginger and cassia. On river banks, he saw them hunt for crocodiles by planting spikes in the ground on which they walked so that they were cut up alive: their bile was used in medicine for mad dogs' bite, carbuncles and pustules, and their flesh was eaten. Oh, he ate it too, and drank hot rice wine with them.

'He bought Tibetan horses with clipped tails and rode them as they did – with stirrups long enough to stand up in so he could shoot his arrows from horseback. Horsemanship was most highly regarded all over Tibet, and then sports of the chase. Fortunately, he was good at both.

'He went to Lhasa, saw the Potala. There he collected scrolls, bronzes, carpets – ' she touched the silent Buddha with a long finger – 'and there he ran into the strangest people of all, lamas and sorcerers . . .'

Raka, her chin cupped in her hand, devoured her words in silence, oblivious now of the rain.

'Sorcerers with the strangest powers. They could do magic: they could make idols speak, turn day into night...'

'How!' burst out Raka, in exclamation rather than questioning.

'How? Oh, how could I tell you that? Even he couldn't explain it. But he told us he saw how darkness could fall at midday, the sky turn ashen, the sun disappear, all birds and animals fall silent as the earth lay in a vast shadow till the sorcerer lifted his hand, spoke magic words and made it vanish.

'Stranger still, they could cause tempests to rise out of a clear, sunlit day. Sudden winds would blow, strong enough to rip tents out by their pegs and break the horses' tetherings, and lightning would flash and thunder roll. It was a sport to the sorcerers, nothing more, but the people would fall flat on their faces and pray, in fear. My father watched it all, you know, he told us about it . . .'

'Did he write a book?'

'A book?' she laughed. 'Oh no, he was not an academic person at all, not like my husband. He was an explorer, a discoverer. He travelled, hunted, collected exquisite things that he eventually brought home to us.' She stared at the bare walls of Carignano. 'It is a pity I have none, or only so few, of his belongings. We were a large family – they were scattered. One of my brothers went to Mauritius, you know, another to Ceylon. And my sisters were all great collectors – in their homes you would see *tankhas*, human hip-bone trumpets, carpets and furs. All I have kept is – this.'

Both gazed at the Buddha, sole survivor of that splendour, looking as though the holocaust around him was less than the dust to him.

Chapter 16

Then Nanda Kaul went on, raising her voice above the drumming of the rain on the roof and the booming and echoing of thunder in the hills that followed the rain like hunting horns.

'The house I had in the plains was crowded, too crowded – my parents' things, my husband's things, his family's. There were Persian carpets his father had bought in Iran when he was with the Ambassador there. There was glass his mother had bought in Venice. There were the Moghul miniatures my husband collected.' She covered her eyes, as though dazzled, and bent her head.

The thunder galloped across the roof, chasing the fleecy clouds and the lightening rain.

'It was too much, you know, Raka. I am not a collector myself. I had to break free of it. So I came to Carignano without any of it.'

'Left it behind?'

'No, no, I gave up the house – it went to the next Vice-Chancellor. No, I distributed it all – to your grandmother, her sister and brothers. I haven't even seen any· of it for years,' she wound up quickly, seeing Raka twist restlessly on her stool, her interest lost in this talk of belongings rather than happenings. Opening out her hands as though willingly releasing the child, she got up brusquely and went to the window. 'There, it's slowing down,' she said, and Raka jumped up and joined her.

'Look at the hydrangeas, beaten down by the rain,' said Nanda Kaul, her voice natural once more, and rounded with relief and pleasure. 'Look how the rain brings out their colour. They're blue again.'

In a little while they went out onto the veranda – on the way, Nanda Kaul picked up *The Travels of Marco Polo* and slid it back onto a bookshelf – and saw the last raindrops slanting down in the sudden, washed sunlight.

The storm was over. The clouds disappeared: one wisp after another was folded up and whisked away into the blue, and a lovely evening emerged, lucid and peerless, the hills fresh and moist and wooded, blue and green like coils of paint out of a tube. Away in the north the rock-scarred snow range glittered. To the south many hundreds of miles of the plain were visible, streaked with streams and pitted with bright pools of rain.

Going down into the garden, Nanda Kaul said, in a voice that was incredibly altered, that was hoarse with a true remembrance, 'How funny, Raka, I just remembered how your mother, when she visited me here as a little girl, used to sing "Rainy days are lily days! Rainy days are lily days!"'

'Lily days?' said Raka, puzzled. 'What did she mean?'

'You'll see,' Nanda Kaul said, and her face twisted oddly at the thought of the blue letter folded up inside her desk. 'Go now, go for your walk,' she said, harshly.

Chapter 17

Next morning Raka saw what her mother, as a child, had meant as soon as she woke up and looked out of the window. At first she mistook them for sheets of pink crêpe paper that someone had crumpled and carelessly flung down the hillside, perhaps after another astonishing party at the club. A moment later she remembered her great-grandmother's words and saw that they were hosts of wild pink zephyranthes that had come up in the night after the first fall of rain.

At breakfast they met over a big milk-jug that Ram Lal had filled with these lilies and set on the table. They were still slick with rain and brought in with them a sharp odour of moist earth. Vividly pink, their heads stood stiffly on the crimson stalks crammed into the milk-jug's neck. Saffron pollen sprinkled the white tablecloth. A child might have drawn them, with pink and yellow wax crayons.

Nibbling toast, Raka asked 'Did my mother often come here when she was little?'

'No,' answered Nanda Kaul, slowly. 'Not often. Your grandmother took her mostly to Simla or Mussoorie – livelier places, you see.'

'Didn't she like it here?'

'Your mother? I think she did,' Nanda Kaul said carefully, not liking to admit that she could scarcely tell one grandchild from the other: the incident of the lilies after rain was the sole one she could remember in connection with Raka's mother. She tried to recall if Tara had gone out to collect lilies, like Ram Lal. She could not. She could only remember the child dashing out of the house after the rain, crying with delight.

'A letter came,' Raka said suddenly, cracking the piece of toast in two. 'Was it from her?'

'No,' said the old lady, her face growing narrower, greyer. 'It was from your grandmother.'

'Did she say anything about Mama?' Raka asked, cautiously casual.

'She's ill again,' Nanda Kaul had to reply, briefly, as she pushed away her cup of coffee. 'She's in a nursing home again, in Geneva.'

In the silence that followed, Nanda Kaul bitterly cursed

her failure to comfort children, her total inability to place herself in another's position and act accordingly. Fantasy and fairy tales had their place in life, she knew it so well. Why then did she tell the child the truth? Who wanted truth? Who could stand it? Nobody. Not even herself. So how could Raka?

But Raka did not say anything more. Her face was pale, but composed. She might have been indifferent, although deliberately so. After all, she had known her mother ill for most of her life, mysteriously ill, mostly in bed, under a loose pink blanket that smelled of damp, like the lilies. It was no new shock. Her voice had something flat about it, Nanda Kaul noted, when she got up, saying 'I think I'll go out now, Nani.'

The old lady nodded, partly in relief and partly in disappointment.

Chapter 18

Raka sprang from the house as if shot out by a gun. She was going to the burnt house on the hill – she would go, she would go alone, no one would stop her, no one would come with her. She sped along the Upper Mall.

Then scrambled up the steep hill, letting loose small avalanches of pebbles and gravel under her toes, making newts dash, lizards slip and tree-crickets crackle. She struggled through the wild rose tangle, their grasping hips and briars, skirted the nettles and the agaves with their sharp sawtooth spines, and flew over the clumps of pink zephyranthes that waved everywhere, risen from the stones like miracles, triumphant for the day.

At the top of the hill was the burnt house she had come to visit. It was only the charred shell of a small stone cottage. The veranda roof was already torn off and flung onto the hillside, the paving stones of the floor were cracked and gaping. The doors swung rotten, the window-frames hung askew, shattered glass lay amongst the cinders. The stairs were a tumble of rocks and weeds. She climbed over them and stood still in the scorched, empty room, gazing up at the sagging roof that dipped lower every day, and listened to the murmuring, sickening silence with the taut expression of one waiting for an explosion.

Further up the ridge, on another knoll, was a house for which stones had been bought and heaped but which had never been built, so that they lay stacked under the wind-stripped pines, lichen creeping over them like a shroud. It was said that the owners of the land had been frightened off by the forest fire that had razed the small cottage and so abandoned the building of it. No one ever came here but Raka and the cuckoos that sang and sang invisibly. These were not the dutiful domestic birds that called Nanda Kaul to attention at Carignano. They were the demented birds that raved and beckoned Raka on to a land where there was no sound, only silence, no light, only shade, and skeletons kept in beds of ash on which the footprints of jackals flowered in grey.

This hill, with its one destroyed house and one unbuilt one, on the ridge under the fire-singed pines, appealed to Raka with the strength of a strong sea-current – pulling, dragging. There was something about it – illegitimate, uncompromising and lawless – that made her tingle. The scene of devastation and failure somehow drew her, inspired her.

Not so the nurseries and bedrooms of her infancy, with their sickly-sweet smells of illness, sadness, drink, medication, milk and tension. Not so the clubs and parks of the

90

cities in which she had lived but to which no one had given her the necessary pass, the key.

Carignano had much to offer – yes, she admitted that readily, nodding her head like a berry – it was the best of places she'd lived in ever. Yet it had in its orderly austerity something she found confining, restricting. It was as dry and clean as a nut but she burst from its shell like an impatient kernel, small and explosive.

It was the ravaged, destroyed and barren spaces in Kasauli that drew her: the ravine where yellow snakes slept under grey rocks and agaves growing out of the dust and rubble, the skeletal pines that rattled in the wind, the wind-levelled hill-tops and the seared remains of the safe, cosy, civilized world in which Raka had no part and to which she owed no attachment.

Here she stood, in the blackened shell of a house that the next storm would bring down, looking down the ravine to the tawny plains that crackled in the heat, so much more intense after the rain, and where Chandigarh's lake lay like molten lead in a groove. She raised herself onto the tips of her toes – tall, tall as a pine – stretched out her arms till she felt the yellow light strike a spark down her fingertips and along her arms till she was alight, ablaze.

Then she broke loose, raced out onto the hillside, up the ridge, through the pines, in blazing silence.

'Cuck-oo – cuck-oo,' sang the wild, mad birds from nowhere.

The caretaker of the burnt house, coming out of a tin shed with a tin mug in his hand, saw her running. 'The crazy one,' he muttered. 'The crazy one from Carignano.'

Chapter 19

The pink lilies folded up and disappeared. The plains were swallowed up by the yellow dust again. The sun frizzled the grasses and blazed on the rocks of Kasauli. All was either bleached or blackened by heat and glare.

'People wonder sometimes,' said Nanda Kaul in that unusually high-pitched voice that made Raka feel strangely itchy, 'what I see in this dry, dusty, dull little place. Kashmir, where I lived as a child, was so different, you know.' She didn't look at Raka but knew the child had lifted her face and was listening. 'It is the water that makes the difference – the streams lined with poplars, gushing white over cold stones, the lakes reflecting the willows, the rivers with houseboats lined along their banks. Everywhere, water. It rules the lives of those who live in Kashmir.'

'Did you live in a houseboat?' asked Raka, lifting bunches of dusty hair from her ears – it was growing long and lay hot and thick on her neck.

'No, of course not,' said Nanda Kaul, elegantly eating a pear. 'Houseboats are only for tourists. We had a proper house, on the banks of the Dal Lake. But we rowed about the lake in shikaras – light little boats, even children of four and five can row them – and do. In summer, yes, we did take a houseboat. When our relations came up from Lucknow and Allahabad, we would engage a houseboat, or sometimes two, and have them punted to Nagin Lake. It was even lovelier there than on the Dal – with orchards and saffron fields coming down to the water's edge, and the cherries ripe at that time of year. We would fish in the lake and ride through the orchards, picking cherries as we went. For picnics we would row in shikaras to the Shalimar or Nishat gardens and drink tea out of samovars on the lawns beside the fountains. It was, I can tell you, a different world from Kasauli,' she ended on a note of surprise.

Raka's words did not reflect the poetry of this vision. They were blunt and straight. 'Why did you come here then,' she asked, 'instead of going back to Kashmir?'

Nanda Kaul simply shook her head and seemed to wander in a field of grey thoughts, alone. 'One does not go back,' she said eventually. 'No, one doesn't go back. One might just as well try to become young again.'

'Would you like that?' pursued Raka, which was unlike her, but then, Nanda Kaul had provoked her.

So Nanda Kaul felt bound to answer. Laughing, she said 'No. No, I don't think I would. I don't think I'd find it – quite safe.'

'But you had such good times, in Kashmir.'

'Yes, yes.' The old lady's eyes flashed. 'What splendid times. There was a stream, you know, at the back of the house, lined with poplars and willows, where our ducks and geese swam. Before the rains, it was shallow, we could paddle in it. Sometimes the ducks swam too far downstream, into other people's gardens and we'd go and fetch them. In the rains, the stream would fill and sometimes overflow into the garden so that the back door opened onto a lake. The adults would cry and worry, the children splash and laugh.

'All round the house was an orchard. Mostly apple trees, but my father was fond of experimenting – it was another hobby of his, only I hesitate to use the word hobby, for his interest was so passionate and the results so successful. For instance, he grafted a plum tree onto a peach and the result was a most curious and delightful fruit – the skin downy, like a peach, only one bit into it and found it plum.

93

'There were almonds that we ate while they were still green and milky, we hardly let any ripen. That was sad for my mother – she liked to fill her store with sacks full of dried fruits and nuts, enough to last us all through the year and send to our relatives in Allahabad and Lucknow. But we thought green almonds better than ripe ones. Not walnuts, though, no one could eat one unripe. There were just three walnut trees – they grew in a grove by the well – but each one was as big as a house – yes, each was bigger than Carignano, a house of branches and leaves – and we would get sackfuls of nuts from them. There was a store room in the house that my mother kept locked but we would creep in if she left it open for a minute, and sit among the sacks and eat our fill of almonds, walnuts, pistachios and chilgoza nuts. There were all kinds of things there – *gucchi*, those curly black dried mushrooms, you know, and dried apricots and raisins. You could say the store room held a fortune, a small fortune. Certainly it was the fortune my mother cared for most. I don't think the orchard meant anything to her but as a provider of that fortune.

'Not to my father. He was adventurous, Raka, adventurous. He did not like being in the house at all. Even when he had to do some paper work – and normally he left it to his overseer – he would have his table and chair taken out under the walnut trees, near the well. He could keep his eye on the estate from there and not feel confined. He was happy travelling, exploring. His interests were so much wider, and his collections reflected them.

'I will tell you now what he liked *best* in the house,' said Nanda Kaul, lowering her eyes on Raka who was growing restive, finding this luncheon too tiresomely drawn out.

Until now they had eaten their meals together in a kind of secretive hurry, each eager to set off in another direction, alone. But now Nanda Kaul seemed unwilling to stop talking, to let Raka out of her sight. There she flopped on her chair, the child, a small fish gasping for its native air, but the old lady had her on the hook – a sharp, bright hook – and held the string tight. As Raka tore at it in impatience, the old lady tightened it, drew her in, reluctant to let go.

She put her long hands down on the table as inspiration descended.

'His private zoo,' she said solemnly, and was gratified to see Raka glance at her – a bit suspiciously but still, her eyes gave that flick of interest as of a fish wheeling around when it spotted bait. 'Yes, animals too he collected, I forgot to tell you,' Nanda Kaul laughed out with relief. 'Oh, the house in Kashmir was full, full of animals, the strangest ones. He had a bear, you know, a great big Himalayan bear that he had found as a cub in the forest when he was out hunting. The cub grew and grew and was enormous by the time I can remember – too enormous for its cage, a huge, shaggy fellow with a white horseshoe on its black chest. But there was nothing my father could do about it – there was no zoo in Kashmir that he could give it to, and he could not set it loose in the forest. It had lost its fear of human beings, you see, and might have strayed into villages for food and frightened, perhaps mauled, the villagers. So there it lived, in our house, in a cage, like a pet King Kong.'

'In a cage, always?'

'Well, my father would let it out on a long iron chain sometimes, but of course only he dared do so, and then it would drive the dogs mad. They would have to be locked upstairs whenever the bear was let out. They were hunting dogs, big wild mastiffs, and could not stand the sight or smell of bear.'

'What would have happened if you had let them together?' asked Raka, slitting her eyes.

'Oh, a massacre – there would have been a massacre,' said Nanda Kaul, not pleased with the expression on the child's face.

The subject of the bear now seemed exhausted and Raka slipped one leg off the chair in readiness to dart but quickly, quickly Nanda Kaul pulled the line tight again.

'It wasn't the wildest creature by any means, or even the smelliest. We had a cage of leopard cats that had that honour. My father said the leopard cats were the fiercest of all creatures, and they never, like the bear, grew accustomed to us. He kept them on the landing, just outside his room, and whenever anyone came near, they'd spit and snarl. Even he could not touch them without leather gloves. He would feed them himself. They loved fish. We used to catch fish in the stream for them, but we never dared feed them ourselves – they had such sudden, vicious claws.'

But Raka seemed not to enjoy the picture of the caged animals devouring the fish. The great-grandmother spotted the hurt in the child's eyes at this picture and abruptly she put another in its place. New as she was to the game, she was becoming an adept, she had a talent, she saw, for giving the child a slide-show, coloured and erratic. One slide would appear upside-down, or there would be a whole series that fluttered past too rapidly to be seen, but now and then one appeared steady, glowing and riveting and then Nanda Kaul straightened up with pride.

'Then there were the peacocks in the garden, Raka, and perhaps they were the only tame creatures we had – nearly tame. You wouldn't have thought so when you heard them screaming like wild things in the orchard, but if they saw us having our meals out on the terrace, in summertime, they would come at a run and peck the rice off our plates, greedily. My mother didn't like that, they broke quite a few plates, but we enjoyed sharing our meals with peacocks,' she laughed.

'And you would have found the lorises sweet, Raka,' she hurried on, with an unaccustomed lightness and dreaminess of tone. 'Of course they slept all day and you had to stay up

96

at night if you wanted to play with them. They were like babies, the way they'd cling to your arm or neck, and their huge, round eyes would shine in the dark as they moved slowly, slowly about the room.'

'In the room?'

'Oh yes, all my father's animals lived inside. I really believe he cared for them as much as for us. Even the pangolin. You wouldn't think anyone could be attached to that hard, scaly creature, always curled up inside its armour, but somehow my father was. He admired it, you see – he admired anything uncommon, extraordinary . . .'

As she murmured on, touching the knives and forks on the table, her eyes wandering in a kind of grey thicket of dreams, the child squirmed, looked over her shoulder at the window, at the sun glistening on the knoll, the pine boughs dipping as the parrots sprang on them, screaming, and longed to get away. She could not understand this new talkativeness of her great-grandmother's who had preferred, till lately, not to talk to her at all, nor had wanted to be talked to. Now she was unable to stop.

But she did, with a start and a look of guilt, as if she had transgressed involuntarily and could not understand her own motive. If Raka had cared to notice, she would have seen a storm of disintegration cross that old, yellowed face with its intricate mapwork of fine lines. But she did not care. She wanted only to go.

They flew apart then, in a kind of anger.

Chapter 20

Nanda Kaul could not let go.

She paced the garden at twilight, the hem of her sari sliding over the pebbles – srr, srr, srr – like a silken snake. She cast her eyes up and down the Mall, waiting to see Raka come dawdling along, tossing a horse chestnut from one cupped hand to another and chanting under her breath.

But Raka did not do that. Instead she came suddenly up over the lip of the gorge, scratched and dusty and breathless. She bit her lip when she found she had bumped into her great-grandmother.

'I never saw a child less like a Raka – a moon,' smiled Nanda Kaul with a smile that was meant to be sweet but which Raka's expression had rendered tart. 'You little jumping thing, you don't come up calmly and shine, do you?'

Raka backed away from her, embarrassed, dubious. But Nanda Kaul began quickly to talk.

'Let us stay here, we'll soon hear the owls,' she said, obliging the child to pace at her side as the garden grew shadowy and still and the hills darkened. The green, glassy sky was full of rooks, searching for a resting place, wheeling in circles, cawing and calling to each other, somehow incapable of settling down for the night.

Nanda Kaul found herself pressing her hands together behind her back in an effort to find some topic that would interest the child. She must not drive her away out of boredom or embarrassment. Somehow, she could not bear to let her slip away. It was as if Raka's indifference was a goad, a challenge to her – the elusive fish, the golden catch.

She found herself talking in a flood again, with a nervous animation and lightness of speech that struck Raka's ear with a false note.

'I kept animals, too, you know, for my children, remembering how much I'd enjoyed having them as a child,' she plunged in recklessly. 'Not only dogs and cats but unusual ones too. Monkeys. We had a pair of monkeys that we kept chained to the veranda rails because they were too destructive to let loose. They were gibbons – long-limbed, black-faced and silvery, like *langurs*, such fun. You could hear them whooping miles away. Your great-grandfather said he could hear them in his office at the other end of the campus, they disturbed him – but he didn't really mind. He knew we enjoyed them, so he let us keep them. The children used to take them for bicycle rides. They had horses, too – your great-grandfather liked them to ride, he thought it good for them and didn't care for the expense. Some of them were really fine horses . . .'

She murmured on, flexing and unflexing her fingers behind her back, and if she had only glanced down and met Raka's eyes then, she would have been halted by something doubting in them, a lack of trust in that clouded look, but some instinct told her not to look into those eyes while she spun her charmed fantasies. She kept her eyes strictly averted from Raka, looking up at the moth-furred sky where the rooks wheeled and cawed, and talked, talked at an exhausting length, till the rooks fell silent, pressed by the darkness into the treetops, and then the owls began to call – softly, experimentally.

'He loved to go riding with the children himself. At that time the campus was surrounded by open fields and you could ride for miles, if you plunged right through the canals and took the footpaths between fields of wheat and sugar-cane and mustard.

'Another thing he got up for the children was a badminton court, and we'd have such games out on the lawn, all of us, at times even by moonlight.'

Just then, as if to illustrate her tale and prove it true, the moon did rise, a great copper-red moon that swelled like a bubble out of the dusk and shone lavishly upon the undulating hills, flooding the valleys and hillsides with such extravagance that the town and village lights grew pale and misty, as if they were under water. Down in the ravine, a pack of jackals was roused to howl lugubriously at the moon and at each other.

Raka turned from the moon – disappointed: she had hoped it was another forest fire.

Trembling inexplicably, the old lady quavered 'We could have anything we wanted of him, anything . . .'

But now Raka sighed and twisted aside to see if Ram Lal would not come and release her from this disagreeable intimacy. He did not come. She would have to do something. She would have to break out into freedom again. She could not bear to be confined to the old lady's fantasy world when the reality outside appealed so strongly.

She thought desperately, with longing, of the charred house on the ridge, of the fire-blasted hilltop where nothing sounded, mercifully, but the creaking of the pines in the wind and the demented cuckoos, wildly calling.

And here she was hedged, smothered, stifled inside the old lady's words, dreams and more words. She yawned with boredom.

'You are tired,' said Nanda Kaul, sadly.

Chapter 21

Raka had given her the slip.

Nanda Kaul moved from one window to the other, mournfully looking out of each pane in turn at the furred yellow mass of afternoon. It was true this was not an hour they normally spent together. Nanda Kaul was supposed to be resting. So was Raka. But when she had peeped in – slyly, slyly – through a crack in the door, she had seen the room empty, the bed flat and untouched. She did not know that the still somnolent afternoon was Raka's best time for exploration, for Raka took care to be back in time for tea. But Nanda Kaul wanted her now, now. She pouted, childishly. One might have said she had arrived at her second childhood if one believed in such things. She looked so exactly like a baby thwarted, wanting attention she did not get, as she stalked through the hot, waiting house.

Then a scream rang through the house, tearing it from end to end. It was the telephone.

Nanda Kaul was obliged to go to it if she did not want the house utterly shredded to bits by its slashing blade. She picked up the receiver with murder in her heart.

It was Ila Das of course. And what was worse – the peremptory shrilling of that instrument, or the gay, mad shrilling of that dreary old friend's voice? One could hardly choose, thought Nanda Kaul, putting her hand to her forehead that had broken into sweat with terror at the sudden screaming.

'I didn't wake you, did I, Nanda? Oh, I do, do hope not, that would be too, too naughty,' warbled Ila Das. 'But you know, I so seldom get at a telephone, I have to seize the opportunity when I can.'

'Where are you now?' asked Nanda Kaul tiredly, and lowered herself onto a chair to stop the bumping of her knees.

'Guess!' shrieked Ila Das. 'Do try and guess!'

'Oh, Ila, how should I know?'

'You could *see* me, you know, if you went out on your veranda and looked right across at – *now* can you guess?'

'No,' snapped Nanda Kaul.

'But Sanawar of course, dear. I'm having lunch with Miss Wright. Have you met Miss Wright, the head of the Home Science department here?'

'No.'

'But you must, you'll be so amused, she's so gay, Miss Wright –'

'Ila,' interrupted Nanda Kaul tersely, 'I have my great-grandchild staying with me, you know. At my age, I really find that quite enough.'

'But of course,' shrilled Ila Das, fluttering up like a shot crow. 'I hadn't forgotten about her, dear, but I wanted to leave you alone a while, just to let her settle down. *Now*, my dear, I can't bottle myself up any longer. I *must* come and see her. Asha's child, isn't she?'

'Asha's *grandchild*.'

'Of course, of course, I hadn't forgotten at all. Now what I was going to suggest, dear . . .' and the voice ran through a series of engagements, meetings and assignations that Nanda Kaul made no effort to follow. She held the receiver away from her ear and mopped her face and tried to blink a kind of grey film out of her eyes. She ought to have had her afternoon rest, she told herself, no matter how uncomfortably warm the bed and troublesome the flies. At her age, it was clear, that hour's rest was more important than running

102

after a child who seemed quite independent enough to look after herself.

She cut off Ila Das's endless burble with an abrupt 'Well, come to tea then. When can you come? Tomorrow?'

'Tomorrow? Tomorrow!' shrieked Ila Das. 'Oh no, no, Nanda dear – you simply have no idea how my days are spent, how full, how busy, how impossible – tomorrow, did you say?' she laughed hectically, then said suddenly in what was, for her, a quiet little voice, 'Yes, well, tomorrow then. May I come at five?'

Nodding wearily, Nanda Kaul rang off before that tiresome friend's voice could take off on another crazed flight.

She went and sat on the veranda rather than return to the bed which the flies had taken over in any case, happily burbling and nuzzling and sticking to the white cotton.

She hoped to catch a glimpse of Ram Lal and tell him to bring the tea early. She would ask for lemon tea today. She thought of lemon tea, of its reviving tartness and clarity in one hot cup after another.

Raka would come to tea. Where was Raka? Fretfully, she looked out over the still, empty garden in which cicadas audibly sizzled as though the sun were frying them in its great golden pan. The child was not there, was never there. She did not like being in Carignano. Perhaps she would not leave her the house after all. Why should she? Raka no more needed, or wanted, a house than a jackal did, or a cicada. She was a wild creature – wild, wild, wild, thought Nanda Kaul.

Perhaps she ought to have refused to have her. Perhaps she ought to leave the house to Tara who needed shelter, a cave to crawl into and die. Perhaps, perhaps . . . the alternatives were as many and as bothersome as flies. Nanda Kaul brushed them aside.

She looked over the dazed, hazy hilltops to Sanawar that lay as trim and neat as ever in its green treetops. Closer to her, the hoopoe promenaded under the apricot trees,

103

smartly furling and unfurling the striped fan on top of its head. Its young had flown and it appeared to be celebrating, even flaunting its independence, its new youth and freedom. It pounced upon a grasshopper and stabbed it to death with its victorious beak.

Nanda Kaul sank lower upon her cane chair. Her heart still bumped inside her as though a string were jerking it. She thought it would be better to have the telephone removed than risk another shock. Strip the house, clear out the telephone, its looped black wires and unforgivable shrieks. Clear the house, leave it bare, silent and restful, thought Nanda Kaul.

A pulse beat in her temple, purple and bulbous. She thought of how she had filled, not this house but the other, earlier ones, for Raka's amusement – with furniture, treasures, trophies, even, dear God, with a zoo. She shrivelled up in her chair with horror at the thought and relaxed only when she recalled, with dignity, that she had not done that to Carignano. Even when at her most desperate to beguile Raka, she had not used, or misused, Carignano, for that shameful purpose. Carignano she had kept clean, true, open for the wind to blow through.

Her eyelids drooped. Through her lashes she saw the pine-needles glisten in the sunlight, glisten and glimmer on top of the knoll, shimmer and scintillate over the garden gate.

Clear the house. Clear it of Raka? No, not that. Of herself? Yes, soon, soon enough.

PART III

Ila Das leaves Carignano

Chapter 1

Tea was laid on the veranda table. On circles and hollows of china, it lay perspiring under cloths weighed down with embroidery and with beads. The thwarted flies buzzed in dismay, nuzzled the fine cloth for a spot of jam, a flake of cake. Raka sat on her stool with a green plastic fly-swatter and chewed her lip over the problem of whether to swat and flatten a bun or not to swat and let the creatures' snorkels pierce a pastry.

Her great-grandmother paced the waved tiles, hands behind her back, murmuring angrily 'She'll be late of course, and I do want my tea. She might think how much I want my tea. But she'll be late, Ila, when was she not?'

For once Ram Lal was watchful, too, squatting outside the kitchen door, watching the path that wound through the chestnut trees to the gate, listening to his black kettle whistle and bump on the fire, prepared to seize it and pour it out onto the crisp tea-leaves the minute he saw the visitor trip up the Mall in the white dust.

Commotion preceded her like a band of *langurs*. Only it took the form of schoolboys who were unfortunately let out from school at just the same time as Ila Das was proceeding towards Carignano with her uneven, rushing step, in her ancient white court shoes, prodding the tip of her great brown umbrella into the dust with an air of faked determination. Like *langurs*, the boys swung about her, long-armed, careless, insulting. They hooted at her little grey top-knot that wobbled on top of her head, at her spectacles that

107

slipped down to the tip of her nose and were only prevented from falling off by an ancient purple ribbon looped over her ears, at the grey rag of the petticoat that gaped dismally beneath the lace hem of her sari – at everything, in short, that was Ila Das. Whooping and hooting, munching and mooing, they ran to the right and left of her, suddenly stopping, suddenly swerving to bump into her small, brittle person, to send her crocheted and motheaten shoulder bag flying or her umbrella spinning. Retrieving it, she shook it at them and made the mistake of opening her mouth. She said only harmless things like 'I'll tell your teacher – I know your Principal, he's a friend of mine – I'll tell him about you . . .' but no matter what she had said, it would have made them bellow – that was the way her voice acted upon everyone.

'Memsahib going to a party,' chanted one flop-haired monkey with a catapult.

'Lace-y and tart-y,' bawled another whose weapon was a marble as large as a horse chestnut.

'Silence, you *bandars*,' screamed Ila Das, and suddenly opened out her umbrella and made to charge through them with it held before her, a torn silk barricade with, she thought, appropriately sharp spikes.

Alas, the spikes were broken. The umbrella squeaked in protest. Boys fell upon it, brought it down into the dust and it bowled along the gravel, kicked helpfully on by them to the side of the road. If there hadn't been a fence there, it would have gone over the edge and rolled down, down, down to the bitter bottom of the *khud* – a sad balloon inflated with Ila Das's dreary past. Roaring in joyous expectation, the boys tried to help it through the rails but it stuck fast, protesting like a lady in hoop-skirts at their uncouth sport.

Ila Das squeaked and shrilled like an agitated shrew, her little eyes blinking tearfully behind the spectacles.

'Hooligans,' she hiccuped, her voice breaking. 'I'll go straight to the Principal. I'll report to the police . . .

At this there was a roar and the band parted and fell aside, leaving the old umbrella stuck helplessly between two rails from which undignified position it was rescued by Ram Lal, who had come marching down the path in policeman-sized strides, sent by Nanda Kaul who stood at the top of the hill by the gate, watching the scene with a frown of disgust.

'*Badmash! Badtameez!*' roared Ram Lal in thundering tones and, extricating the umbrella now as maimed and crooked as a hunchback, a witch of olden times tied and readied for the fatal dip in the pond, flourished it at their quickly retreating, torn, patched and impertinent behinds. Once safely down the road, the boys began to whoop and whistle again, doubling up and playing leap-frog in delight.

But neither Ram Lal nor Ila Das glanced at their high jinks. Rolling up the tired and rusty umbrella, Ram Lal handed it to Ila Das with some disdain.

'Thank you, Ram Lal,' she piped and, hitching up the sari above her stockinged ankles, began to climb the steep, gravelly path between the chestnut trees to Carignano. Following her, Ram Lal could hear the rapid, shallow breathing, like an old animal that has been made to run before the hounds. Carefully turning his head, he spat into the raspberry bushes. She'd need her tea, he'd better hurry, he thought.

Chapter 2

But Ila Das was accustomed to such scenes: she could no more have gone down the road to post a letter without being pursued, or obstructed, by just such a jeering mob as had escorted her to Carignano today, than royalty could have proceeded in a golden carriage without crowds to wave it and cheer it on its way. All her life mobs had taunted and derided her. Why, thought Nanda Kaul, impatiently waiting beneath the smiling, scoffing pine trees, when Ila Das was a baby in a pram, exactly such a mob must have surrounded her, snatched away her rattle and made her squeak and shrill just as she had on the dusty road to Carignano.

It was hard to picture Ila as an infant, true. In an attempt to do so, Nanda Kaul saw the shrivelled old lady in miniature, propped up against lace-edged pillows in a sky-blue pram, just as she was now only without the shining porcelain dentures.

About the pram and the laces she was certain. Nanda Kaul's family had known Ila Das's in the days when some of the glory of the British Empire was allowed to reflect on a few favoured natives. Such families lived in large bungalows on quiet roads. In their houses, sherry was served before lunch, port after. Their servants wore white cotton gloves. The ladies went for evening drives along the river, at first in creaking carriages, later in pompously purring automobiles. So of course there had been a sky-blue perambulator, too, and an ayah to push it importantly along under the jacaranda trees, and a skirted nanny to time its promenade on a great china-saucer watch presented to her by her employers.

This was the contradiction in Ila Das's life that irked Nanda Kaul – it was the piece of gravel that insisted on slipping into her shoe and out of it. Ila Das's life was simply not all of a piece – Nanda Kaul had seen so many pieces of it, littered over the northern plains, and here was the last broken bit, spiked by an agave beside the path leading to Carignano.

Ram Lal hurried to help the old lady off the pointed spike,

putting her into a flutter of shrill thanks that carried all the way up to the gate like the cackle of an agitated parrot.

It was this cackle, this scream of hers, Nanda Kaul thought, that held all the assorted pieces of her life together like a string or chain. It was the motif of her life, unmistakably. Such a voice no human being ought to have had: it was anti-social to possess, to emit such sounds as poor Ila Das made by way of communication.

Strange to think there was an infant once who, when lisping the nanny-goat-and-pinafore rhymes that western and westernized babies speak, curdled the blood of the adults who dandled her on their knees. But one could imagine – Nanda Kaul narrowed her eyes as she stared down at the bald white scalp, bent to the task of struggling uphill in the afternoon heat – Ila Das as an infant in an afternoon frock of blue ribbons and white lace, screeching the most unimaginably horrid sounds that sent shivers down the spines of guests and relatives invited to hear her recite her nursery rhymes.

Nanda Kaul could not only imagine it, she could remember the time. She and Ila Das had played together as children, children's games like Oranges-and-Lemons and cooking dolls' meals under the *gol-mohur* trees, with scarlet blossoms and yellow pods for food.

They had gone to school together, solemnly cycling down the quiet roads to the convent, while the happily illiterate urchins cheered them, yelling 'Parr-ot, parr-ot, sing to us!' Ila Das would be primly silent on her splendid silver Raleigh, biting her lip in terror of being knocked down in the road.

In school, alas, she had to speak. Teachers shivered, their teeth on edge, as if a child had squeaked a pencil on a slate or slid a nail down a glass-pane, while children clapped their hands over their mouths, making giggles burst forth the more rudely when Ila Das stood up, almost prancing on her

111

tiptoes, to recite The Boy Stood On The Burning Deck.
Hurriedly teachers hushed her, begged her to give others,
with normal growls and mutters for voices, a chance. And
poor Ila had learnt the whole poem through, wanted so
much to recite it all. Yet she had to bottle up that voice with
a hiccup and sit down, fizzing and burbling impotently, her
hands in her lap, while others muttered and floundered
through a parody, a pretence of the verse.

In distress, her parents bought her a piano and engaged a
new governess, one who could teach Ila to play. Perhaps
they hoped to silence the child at parties by giving her pieces
to play rather than recite. Nanda Kaul's hands rose involuntarily to her ears under the loops of white hair, as she
recalled those tea-parties and the appalling, the unendurable
sounds made by little Ila Das, pigtails bouncing jollily on
her back, as she tinkled on the piano keys as if rummaging
amongst a bagful of china, hogs' tusks and clapping
dentures, her voice raised like a tom-cat's in battle, yowling

> 'Darling, I am growing *old*!
> Silver threads among the *gold* . . .'

Here she came, Ila Das, still little Ila Das, with what
remained of the pigtail wound on top of her head like a
tea-cosy, an egg-cosy, yellowed rather than whitened by
age, and Nanda Kaul looked down from her height, having
invited her to tea, having failed to put her away out of sight
and mind. Here she was, that last little broken bit of a crazy
life, fluttering up over the gravel like a bit of crumpled
paper.

'Ila,' she sighed, bending to swing open the unwilling
gate, 'come'.

And Ila, screwing up her little button eyes with delight at
seeing Nanda Kaul – for all through her ragged life Nanda
Kaul had been there, standing at a height, like a beacon, like
an ideal – and stepping eagerly in, flung herself upon her

friend and pecked and pecked her cold, flat cheek, crying
little hideous cries of delight and love into the cringing ears.

Chapter 3

'Darling,' screeched Ila Das, 'darling, what sort of a summer has it been? Why haven't we met earlier, oftener? My,
and we're neighbours – you in your manorial hall and I in
my village hut down below. I've so much to *tell*, Nanda –
and you? And you?'

But Nanda Kaul would not stand at the gate and perform
a comedy for the benefit of the urchins – she knew where
they hid, watching, behind the agaves and the bushes of
Spanish broom. Giving them a withering look, she took Ila
firmly by the elbow and turned her towards the house
where Raka stood teetering on the edge of the veranda,
curious to see the maker, the perpetrator of such unholy
sounds.

Suddenly Ila Das gave the crooked umbrella a merry
swing – a swing that belonged to a park on a Sunday
afternoon, when the band played, the merry-go-round
revolved and flowers sprang to attention in their beds all
around – and gave a little hop, then clutched Nanda Kaul's
arm in its long sleeve of silk that buttoned at the wrist with
two opals, and said 'Ooh, look, those lovely apricot trees.
Did they bear a good crop, Nanda? Did you make that
delicious jam? Mmm, when I think of it . . .' a naughty pink
tongue crept over the lips, licking, then departed with a
giggle. 'How lovely the house looks, Nanda. *Dear* Carignano. Now if you were to see *my* castle . . .' and she went
into peals of laughter that rang like a fire engine's fatal bell

so that two doves, amazed, shot out of the trees and vanished, and even Raka took a startled step backwards.

Ila Das saw the movement of the white dress on the shadowy veranda. Clapping her hand over her mouth, she stood stockstill. 'My,' she breathed, pop-eyed. 'I actually forgot. Only for a moment – but I actually forgot the child, Nanda, in my joy at seeing you again. How could I? How could I?' Shaking her head so that steel pins showered from her small top-knot, she went on, 'Nanda's great-grandchild! Could anyone believe it – looking at you?' She turned to look. 'No,' she decided, 'positively not.'

'But there she is, my great-grandchild,' said Nanda Kaul drily, and called 'Raka.'

Raka put down the fly-swatter and came, dragging her feet and looking her most mosquito-like.

Ila Das made a little tripping rush forwards and, reaching out, captured the hand that hung limply at the side and pumped it up and down with a vigour that Nanda Kaul remembered having seen in the person of her father, a little whiskered gentleman in a smoking jacket who used to insist on shaking hands with every little girl that came to Ila Das's party, making them stumble backwards and titter. Here was Ila Das now, pumping limp Raka's lifeless hand, crying little shrill cries that made her wince and attempt a retreat.

'My dear, you and I are simply bound to be friends, you know, *bound* to be. I've known your great-grandmother for – oh, how many years is it now? Well, I'm not going to bore you by counting them – I'm not really sure I *can* count them –' with a wicked wink magnified to dragonfly proportions by the bi-focal lenses over the eyes –'but when one's known anyone *that* long, you know, one is practically related. Oh, *absolutely* related, and I insist, I simply insist –' the grasp on Raka's shrinking fingers tightened –'on being great grand-aunt to *you*, my dear, dear little girl!' Then she leant forward from the waist – she was only about the same height as

114

Raka, scarcely taller – and pecked her rapidly on the cheek.
'There!' she beamed and released Raka who fell back into
the lilies, slightly gasping and shaking herself as if she felt
her fur, or fuzz, rumpled by contact.

Nanda Kaul stood watching, an ironic twist to her lips.
She herself had never grasped Raka's hand, nor kissed her –
how had Ila Das dared? It had been presumptuous of her –
Raka's unconcealed shudder and sudden whitening of the
lips showed how presumptuous it had been – and Nanda
Kaul both felt for her outrage and exulted in it. At last
someone had swung a net over that crafty little mosquito.

In the background, Ram Lal hovered, waving away flies,
putting down tea pot and milk jug, whisking away beaded
nets to reveal the fruit of his day's unusual labour. It was not
every day they invited someone to tea. Ram Lal had almost
forgotten how to go about it (and Nanda Kaul lifted an
eyebrow in surprise at his idea of tea-party fare) but was
quickly remembering it all now. It was with quite an air that
he drew back the lowest chair for Ila Das and took away her
umbrella, leaving them to the repast with one last look at
Raka, a rather dubious one, as if he couldn't be sure how *that*
one would conduct herself.

Raka quite clearly had no notion how to conduct herself
at a party. She hung about. She hovered over her chair only
to find Ila Das plopping down upon it with a kind of
schoolboy abandon, a schoolboy way of throwing herself
backwards so that her feet flew up in the air, and there they
swung. Even Raka's low chair was too high for those short
legs. An inch or two above the ground those cracked old
court shoes swung to and fro, happily, as if five years old
and at a party once more.

There was some fuss and bother about the cloth shoulder
bag – it was taken off but where was it to be put? Ought it to
be hung? At last a sigh went up and Ila Das let forth again
with a sound that made the hoopoes on the bit of grass take

115

off and flee the garden and the crickets draw in their heads and hide.

Chapter 4

'Mum-mum-mum,' her lips mumbled together, then flapped open across the silky dentures. 'Oh, how this all reminds me of *home*, Nanda. I mean childhood of course, when we had honey for tea and badminton on the lawn after.'

Nanda Kaul lifted that elegant eyebrow again, together with the teapot that had been bought in the bazaar by Ram Lal and was thick, white and cheap. 'I wonder what, in all of Carignano, could remind you of that, Ila,' she said.

'Ooh,' burst Ila Das right into a cupful of hot tea so that it flew up in a spray. 'Ooh, Nanda, the very air, the atmosphere about you brings it all back to me. Why, I see your lovely mother with that beautiful Kashmiri complexion of hers, and the red Brahmin thread looped through her ears, pouring out tea for us and all the little dogs at her feet – how they loved her. We *all* did. And then your father would come in from the orchard, holding one special peach he had plucked for her, and his pockets full of nuts for us, and he'd call us to him and say . . .'

Raka wilted. She hung her arms between her knees and drooped her head on its thin stalk. It seemed the old ladies were going to play, all afternoon, that game of old age – that reconstructing, block by gilded block, of the castle of childhood, so ramshackle and precarious, and of stuffing it with that dolls' house furniture, those impossibly gilded red velvet sofas and painted bedsteads, that always smelt of dust

116

and mice and that she had never cared to play with. She very much wanted to eat her tea, for once to have something to eat at tea, but it seemed she would have to pay for it. She gazed at a small ant under the table, crawling off with a crystal of sugar loaded onto its back, and sighed.

Ila Das heard her sigh and gave a quick bounce on her chair, turned her megaphone upon the child and shrieked 'How you would have loved that house, my dear! It was a children's paradise, you know, a veritable paradise. The minute you stepped in and closed the high gate behind you –' she clapped her hands together with a wooden smack –'you felt yourself in fairyland. Why, you might be taken to pick green chillies in the garden to feed the parrot – very carefully, you know, it nipped horribly – or you might decide to ride your bicycles down the drive, or climb the fig tree and swing in its branches like a band of monkeys. Oh, anything, everything was permitted –'

But still the child's head lolled drearily and the wisps of hair dried to a stiff shade of brown, their tips ending in reddish sparks, swung on either side of the doleful face.

'And particularly the piano!' cried Ila Das, clasping her hands together just under her chin and looking from side to side as though she were peeping at mountains of presents on either side of her. 'After the party games, and the big tea, the piano,' and to Raka's astonishment and Nanda Kaul's horror, Ila Das flung back the lid of an imaginary piano with a flourish as of a magician whisking a silk handkerchief off the magic rabbit, and then plunged into the imaginary keys with both hands splayed, at the same time pumping the imaginary pedals with her little feet and throwing back her head to bellow 'Darling, I am growing o-o-old!'

Nanda Kaul froze into a state of pale concrete. The entire weight of the overloaded past seemed to pour onto her like liquid cement that immediately set solid, incarcerating her in its stiff gloom. She sat with her lips tightly set and her eyes wide open, hardly able to believe in this raucous apparition now ripping into Honeysuckle Rose in a voice like an arrow that pierced Nanda Kaul's temple and penetrated her jaws, setting her teeth tingling.

The arrow withdrew, silence seeped in. But Ila Das's fingers remained splayed across the keyboard, horribly knotted and yellowed, and her feet remained pressed on the pedals. She swayed her head gently on a stalk as though a breeze were rustling by, her button eyes acquired the glaze of old trinkets, and opening her mouth in a round O, she began to quaver

'Ye banks and braes o' bonny Doon,
How can ye bloom sae fresh and fair . . .'

All the pine trees on the knoll shivered and cast their glistening needles in a hushed shower. The cicadas crept under the roasting stones and wept with little susurrating sounds. Pebbles suddenly released their hold on the hillside and went sliding down the ravine in a weeping rush.

On the veranda Raka and her great-grandmother sat stockstill and gaping at Ila Das crooning over the imaginary piano with round glass tears popping out of her little eyes and bouncing across her cheeks and off the tip of her nose.

'How can ye chant, ye little birds,
And I sae weary fu' o' care!'

Then she had to search in her cloth bag for a handker-chief. Whipping it out, she trumpeted into it – a horrendous sound for such a small, shrunken creature to make – and sat back in the low chair, wiping her eyes, hiccuping through the hankie, swinging her legs and smiling 'Aren't I awful – ooh, aren't I just awful!'

Straightening her back centimetre by regal centimetre, Nanda Kaul asked crisply 'Milk or lemon, Ila?'

Chapter 5

Stuffing the handkerchief back into the bag and attacking a plate of hot buttered toast with rapacity, Ila Das threw Raka an arch look and said 'Don't mind me, dear – I'm like that when I get on to music. It played such a role in our lives, didn't it, Nanda? I'm afraid it's all out of fashion now – those sweet songs, those musical soirées at which the family would gather around the piano and sing. A tragedy, I feel, a tragedy,' she proclaimed, and smashed a great piece of toast to bits with her dentures.

'I don't know,' said Nanda Kaul, still very rigid and royal. 'I never cared for music myself. It makes me *fidget*. I greatly prefer silence.'

Ila Das preferred not to hear. She absolutely refused to hear. Sweeping another piece of toast off the platter and into her mouth, she went on through the cement-mixer action of crunching toast, 'No such thing could happen in *your* house, of course, Nanda. That was a tradition you carried on. Oh, the Vice-Chancellor's house –' and she closed her eyes into little bright slits of pleasure – 'that home away from home for me. All the old customs, the old ways, they got a new lease on life in the Vice-Chancellor's house.' Her eyes opened and blazed with admiration, the admiration that Nanda Kaul always struck from her like sparks. 'The last of the gracious old homes, Nanda . . .'

Raka, putting her plate back on the table, the snacks uneaten, gave a little agonized twist of despair, then sat still, limp, faded. It seemed there was no end to this tiresome teatime game of old ladies, no way out of its cobweb maze.

Lately her great-grandmother had bored her with it, played it with such theatrical ardour as to make it as unreal as theatre. It made her ache for the empty house on the charred hill, the empty summer-stricken view of the plains below, the ravine with its snakes, bones and smoking kilns – all silent, and a forest fire to wipe it all away, leaving ashes and silence.

'More tea?' Nanda Kaul murmured to her under cover of Ila Das's waterfall of speech.

She shook her head and glanced at her great-grandmother. She saw tiredness like a grey web across that aged face. It seemed Nanda Kaul herself had tired of her game. She was leaving it to Ila Das.

Ila Das didn't mind. She didn't notice.

'Do you remember what a pest I was, Nanda? How gladly I'd leave my little room in the teachers' hostel – ooh, the noise there, the *noise*! It still rings in my poor ears – and cycle down that beautiful avenue all lined with eucalyptus trees, to the Vice-Chancellor's house. It was so *delicious* to know I had a welcome waiting for me there. Delicious to put away all those books, papers and corrections, just put them away and set off on my cycle to the house that was never, never shut. I could always be sure of finding you on the veranda – tea waiting in winter, lemonade in the summer – pets running free everywhere, the children and their friends playing cricket on the lawn, and all cares could be forgotten for an evening.

'You know, it wasn't easy at that time. To start teaching at the age of forty, Nanda dear, really wasn't so easy. I couldn't seem to control the girls. The teachers seemed – ooh, you know, of a different *class*, Nanda, do you understand me? And my eyes were giving way. And all the family troubles –' a sigh burst from her like air from a slashed balloon and the little body crumpled on its chair. 'But,' she cried out – and a startled bul-bul exploded from the apricot

120

tree – 'there was always the Vice-Chancellor's house, and good use I made of it, didn't I?'

'Ooh,' she quavered, swivelling about to focus on that sullen, unresponsive child, hoping to liven her up for surely the young should be lively; wasn't Ila Das still lively – in spite of everything, still lively? 'You wouldn't believe it, my dear, but I was quite capable of running out on the lawn and taking a cricket bat out of the boys' hands and playing myself.' She beamed over the memory at Raka as if over a lollipop. Raka shuddered at its stickiness. 'In winter, we'd stay indoors and there'd be music. All the girls studied music, your grandmother amongst them,' she twinkled at Raka. 'The piano, the flute, the veena, the sitar – and so many voices singing, in so many languages. Those are memories to treasure,' she hummed as if it were a line from a song – and perhaps it was. 'And your great-grandmother always a picture. No matter how simple the occasion, she was always in silk, always in pearls and emeralds. I wish you *knew* what a picture she was, dear.'

Nanda Kaul sat back in her upright chair and gazed straight at her, in silence. She was not going to help Ila Das play this game. No, it was too shameful. She had decided that it was shameful and that, in any case, it had no appeal for Raka, the child who never played games.

'But the summers were best,' Ila Das burbled on. 'In spite of the heat and dust, summers were best. Those enormous melons that grew in your garden – the children would split them and eat them on the veranda steps. The lichee trees would be loaded, oh *loaded*, with bunches of ripe pink fruit. And the jamun tree – mum, mum,' she gobbled. 'And after the heat of the day, the lovely evenings out on the freshly watered lawn.

'Oh, and the badminton court. What evenings we spent on the badminton court. How all the teachers waited for an invitation to play badminton at the Vice-Chancellor's house. He used to organize matches, you know – your great-grandfather, my dear. We'd play mixed doubles. I remember playing with one of your great-uncles, my dear, against the Vice-Chancellor and Miss David. Miss David was an *ace* player – ooh, she was good – and they beat us hollow . . .'

But the line was cut suddenly as a thread is cut – snip – completely. She was silent.

Raka looked up, hardly able to believe her ears. She saw her great-grandmother carefully build a cage with her long fingers, a cage of white bones, cracking apart. She saw Ila Das sitting silent, her mouth hanging open foolishly – speech had been snatched out of it and whisked away. What sharp, swift scissors had descended on that endless tangle of her game? The badminton court – mixed doubles – Miss David – and here were Ila Das and Nanda Kaul, both beaten, silent.

Chapter 6

Now Nanda Kaul rose and showed the worth of her background, her upbringing. Now was the moment to rise and put all in its place, like the goddess of a naughty land returned to deal with chaos. She had allowed things to get out of hand, to skip and dance and posture too vainly, too grotesquely. Now was the time to silence it, to smooth it away and show her character – how it was made, what made it, how it had lasted. For it had lasted.

'Raka, will you call Ram Lal, please, to take away the tea. The flies are a nuisance,' she said in a clear, crisp tone like the heart of a plant, the icy white centre of it. 'And you must tell

122

me, Ila, what you have been doing with yourself. How is your village work getting on?'

As Raka jumped and ran, stumbling with relief and fear at being caught again, the two women turned to each other with suffering, sobered faces, and when Ila Das spoke again, the acid of truth ran in it, giving her voice a bitter, burnt edge.

Now the pink lichees, the badminton games and piano tunes fled from Ila Das's side, leaving behind a shrivelled, shaking thing. Little by little, all those sweetnesses, those softnesses died or departed, leaving her every minute drier, dustier and more desperate.

Nanda Kaul knew: she had followed this depairing progress from not too great a distance. So Ila Das could turn to her with a harsh honesty that was as real as her memory-making had been, and Nanda Kaul knew how real each was in its turn, how they came together, one bitter, corroded edge joining the other, making up this wretched whole.

By the time Ila Das had come to the university campus as a lecturer in Home Science, at Nanda Kaul's suggestion and Mr Kaul's invitation, those flowery, tinkling years were already over. Her mother lay rotting in bed with a broken hip that would not mend, and her father was dead of a stroke. The family fortune, divided amongst three drunken, dissolute sons as in a story, and not a penny of it to either of the two clever, thrifty, hard-working daughters, Ila and Rima, was then quickly becoming a thing of the past, no longer retrievable, barely believable. The sons had been sent to foreign universities – to Heidelberg, Cambridge, Harvard – and wherever they were, each had contrived not to attend a single lecture, to drink themselves ill, to find the nearest racecourse and squander their allowances on horses that never won. To begin with, their father had paid their debts, then begun to sell his own horses, his carriage, his house, his land. When he died, not one of them came to the

123

funeral. They knew there was nothing left for them to inherit. They pestered their mother and two sisters then, for the last of the jewellery, and soon had them driven out into rented rooms and boarding-houses, finally to whatever roof charity would hold over them. Eventually, blessedly, they died. Or disappeared.

Then Nanda Kaul had watched those two horrifically ugly, hideously handicapped girls show the worth of *their* upbringing, *their* character. She had watched as they shingled their hair, queued up for buses and went to work. Rima, whose piano playing was of a different class from her sister's, had given piano lessons, going from house to house and then coming home to nurse the mother with the rotten hip. As for Ila, there was nothing for it but for Nanda Kaul to suggest to her husband, the Vice-Chancellor, that he create a job for her in the Home Science College. He had been gracious and kindly about it, and it was to this comparatively blessed period of her life, secure for a while as a lecturer, sure of her meals and a bed in the hostel, that Ila Das's jolly talk of badminton doubles and lawn parties belonged.

'I wish,' she sighed now, 'I wish I had stayed there, Nanda. How often I go back to that time and think it over again, and I know now – I know *now* – I should not have been so hotheaded. Ooh, in my position, a little humility would have been much, much better . . .' and she twisted about to fish the handkerchief out of her bag and sniffle in its folds.

'There was no call for humility,' said Nanda Kaul crisply. 'Everybody knew that your experience called for your being made the Principal when Mrs Chatterji retired. Everybody knew the reason you weren't was that the Vice-Chancellor who had appointed you was dead and there was a new Vice-Chancellor to go against his ways and show his strength. How could you stand for that?'

'I didn't, I didn't,' Ila Das cried. 'That was why I resigned, Nanda – it was the only honourable thing to do, wasn't it? But ooh, the flesh is weak, and you know how things have gone for me since then, Nanda. You know how I've had to go from pillar to post, trying to earn fifty rupees here and fifty rupees there, with not a room to call my own most of the time, and it's grown worse and worse . . .'

Nanda Kaul nodded. She knew. She had watched that degrading, hopeless search, for Ila Das was already then close to the official age for retirement and no matter how low she pitched her demands, there were always bright, carefree young girls to be employed for even less. As for qualifications, Ila Das's were of the genteel sort that are not put on paper and rubber-stamped, and she was turned away by the employment bureau and any employer that she nerved herself to face.

For a while her sister had kept her, literally dividing each piece of bread in two between them – fortunately the mother died before she starved – and then Nanda Kaul had heard of the course in social service which, if Ila was willing to take it, would definitely lead to a Government job and with it would go the usual emoluments of pension, provident fund and medical aid that now seemed like pieces of gold to her. She had taken the course, triumphantly collected the rubber-stamped document qualifying her to be a social worker, and arrived in the Himalayan foothills to do her duty amongst the peasants, wood-cutters, road labour and goatherds.

Once again she had strayed into Nanda Kaul's domain – only to find that Nanda Kaul did not rule here; Nanda Kaul had retired.

Chapter 7

She came out of retirement to ask, in a low voice, 'Are you managing, Ila? Can you make ends meet?'

For a while Ila Das snuffled into her handkerchief. Then she folded it up into smaller and ever smaller squares. When it could not be folded any further, she held it tightly in her hand and said 'Not since Rima's troubles grew so bad. You know how it is – young people don't play the piano any more, even in Christian families they go in for the guitar, for pop music – all a closed book to darling Rima, of course. She's lost pupil after pupil, Nanda, and now this cataract of hers makes her totally helpless. I asked Mrs Wright to help her – you remember Mrs Wright, she was – oh, not a governess but a nanny in our house at one time – and has a little flat in Calcutta. Well, she's given Rima her spare bed in a corner of it. I've been sending a tiny sum for her board and lodging – the barest minimum, but oh,' she began to giggle with little spurting, jerking sounds, 'the barest minimum was all I had.'

'But what are you doing about it, Ila? How do you manage?'

'I'm trying, I'm trying,' sang Ila Das, nodding her head so that the top-knot slipped and sank.

Watching from behind the hydrangea bushes, Raka thought of that ball she had seen in the club one night, of the grotesque figures that had jerked and pranced there. It seemed to her that Ila Das was another such puppet, making her own mad music to jerk and prance to. Nibbling at a brown petal, Raka watched through lowered lashes.

Ila Das began to bounce again, as she piped optimistically, 'I've been writing around to magazines and journals. I thought if one of them were interested in a column on home science, I could write one every month – or every week – and perhaps earn twenty or thirty rupees above my salary. Thirty rupees –' her eyes boggled behind the bifocal lenses – 'thirty rupees would cover the cost of feeding me. It would be a *fortune!*' she exploded in a spray of happy spit, and swung her little legs back and forth.

'Isn't it absurd,' she rattled on, 'how helpless our up-bringing made us, Nanda. We thought we were being equipped with the very best – French lessons, piano lessons, English governesses – my, all that only to find it left us helpless, positively *handicapped*.' She cracked with laughter like an old egg. 'Now if I were one of the peasants in my village, perhaps I'd manage quite well. Grow a pumpkin vine, keep a goat, pick up kindling in the forest for fire – and perhaps I could cut down those thirty rupees I need to twenty-five, to *twenty* – but *not*, I think, less.' Almost crying, she turned to Nanda Kaul. 'Do you think I could do with *less*?'

Dumbly, Nanda Kaul shook her head. She held the arm of her chair very tightly in an effort to speak, to say 'Come and stay with me, Ila,' and then clutched it tighter still to keep herself from saying what would ruin her existence here at Carignano. She simply shook her head.

Chapter 8

'Oh, I *do* feel ashamed of myself,' shrieked Ila Das. 'Ooh, I do, when I think how much better off I am than the poor,

poor people around me. Why, you wouldn't believe the things I see, Nanda. It isn't just that I have this little bit of security, this tiny bit of status –' she gave a shout of laughter at herself –'you know, as a welfare officer employed by the Government, while they simply starve if their cow dries up or the weevils destroy their potato crop – but the horrible, horrible degradation in which they live – ooh, Nanda,' her voice plunged down, down into the deepest gloom, 'why then, I *do* see the worth of our kind of upbringing after all. At least one is saved *that* degradation.

'You know, Nanda, I've been brought up a Christian, and to see these poor, ignorant people grovel in the dust before their wretched little oil-smeared, tinsel-decked idols, gives me a *turn*. Ooh, I'll say it does. And that oily, oily priest-man we have slinking about our village – I can tell he's up to no good. I *hate* him!' she suddenly spat out from between her dentures.

Raka, now ambling in the long grass under the apricot trees, stopped and stared at the sound of that fierce spitting.

'Oh, how I *hate* him! *He*'s responsible for that lovely Maya-devi's little son dying. Did I tell you, Nanda? The little boy was playing barefoot in the lane as these children do, and cut his foot on a rusty nail. I *told* Maya-devi to take him to the clinic straightaway for an anti-tetanus, but she wouldn't hear of it. Or, rather, the priest-man wouldn't hear of it. Nooo, he said, Nooo, injections were the work of the devil and Maya-devi was *not* to take the child to the clinic. Well,' she went on, 'that little boy died, of course, and you know what it is to die of tetanus. Now Maya-devi knows.'

She was a dramatic raconteur: it took nerve to listen to her relate the hair-raising stories of her experiences as a welfare officer, and Nanda Kaul sat straighter and stiffer than ever, as if horror were slowly paralysing her.

'And, Nanda, if you only *saw* the havoc played amongst

the children by conjunctivitis and trachoma, how many of them are doomed to blindness! But will they believe me when I tell them they need to go to the clinic for treatment? No. My dear, a handful of red chilli powder is considered treatment enough, or a pack of cowdung, or – or – oh, I shan't harrow you with details. I do believe the women would listen to me if it weren't for that *impossible* priest. It's so much harder to teach a man anything, Nanda – the women are willing, poor dears, to try and change their dreadful lives by an effort, but do you think their men will let them? Nooo, not one bit.

'Now I've run into all this trouble over trying to stop child marriage. That is one of the laws of the land, isn't it, and aren't I there to enforce the law? Isn't that what I'm paid for by the Government? Well, so I go along my way, trying to do my duty, going from house to house and especially wherever I hear there's a child marriage in the offing, and *threaten* them and tell them how they can go to prison for committing a social offence. I do think the women would listen to me – if anyone knows what it is for a girl to be married and bear children at the age of twelve, it's them, isn't it? But wherever I go, the priest follows me, and undoes what I do. He *hates* me, Nanda – ooh, he *hates* me.'

'Ila,' said Nanda Kaul, stirring uneasily, 'Ila, do be careful.'

Ila Das cackled with laughter, swung her legs and thwacked her hands together. 'Careful? You don't think he frightens me, do you? That old goat? No, nooo, not in the least. But he's wicked, wicked. He sets the young men in the village against me, too. And how can I get my work done if even the young men don't take my side and help? In the end, the women listen to *them* – if not to the priest, then definitely to their husbands.

'Now I've just heard about a family living in my own village – they're planning to marry their little girl, who is

129

only just seven, to an old man in the next village because he owns a quarter of an acre of land and two goats. He's a widower and has six children but, for a bit of land and two goats, they're willing to sacrifice their little girl, Nanda, can you believe it? I've argued and argued with her mother, and I even tackled the father, Preet Singh, in the potato fields the other day. But he's a sullen lout, I could see I wasn't making any headway with him.

'Ooh, dear, so it goes,' she wound up, silenced by despondency and by Ram Lal's appearance on the scene.

Chapter 9

He had been lighting the *hamam* to heat Raka's bath water and had not bothered to come earlier. Now he busied himself, taking off the fly-specked nets, piling the crockery on a wooden tray, shaking out the folds of the aged table-cloth that cracked with stiffness, while the two ladies discussed the weather in his presence, as they had been taught to do, wondering aloud when the hot spell would end and the monsoon come.

'It's so dry, so dry, I hardly dare light a match for fear it will all go up in flames,' said Ila Das, getting up and looking for her bag. 'A forest fire is more than even a Government welfare officer can tackle,' she laughed, and searched for her umbrella.

In the midst of this no one noticed Raka. Raka had scrambled up to the top of the knoll, grasping at weeds and slipping on the dry pine-needles, till she had drawn herself up to the rocks under the pine trees. For a while she sat there, chin on her knees, looking out on the hills that flowed, wave on wave, to the horizon, and listened to the wind that blew up and crashed into the pines, then receded and went murmuring away like the sea. She narrowed her eyes and the greys and blues of the scene melted together, till waves and hills, sea and wind were all one. She was in a boat, rocking, alone.

Then there was a little movement in front of the house. There were Ila Das and Nanda Kaul coming down the steps from the veranda, from under the apricot trees, and strolling down the flagged path to the gate – Nanda Kaul rigidly straight, her movements silken and silver, while little Ila Das bobbed up and down beside her, swinging her cloth bag, waving her umbrella and making her top-knot dance.

Crouching under the pines, Raka watched them progress unevenly down to the gate. Then, sliding her legs out from under her, she glanced back at the veranda and saw that Ram Lal was still there, busily sweeping up crumbs, swatting flies and stacking plates. With a sudden spring, she rose and went flying down the knoll, the bright sparks at the ends of her dry hair flying like flames in the wind, dashed round the *hamam* and dived into the kitchen.

There she paused, letting her eyes get used to the thick, smoky darkness. When they could see, she put out her hand and snatched up the box of matches from the table and dropped it into her pocket.

She emerged casually, hands behind her back, a little stiff. She glanced again to see if Ram Lal were coming, then to see if the ladies had parted. No, they were still at the gate, nattering. One quick dart and, lizard-like, she was over the fence and had dropped down the lip of the ravine and vanished. She could only be heard leaping and sliding down amongst the rolling pebbles and gravel, but there was no one to hear.

Chapter 10

'So, Ila,' said Nanda Kaul, placing one hand on the gate and pressing gently, unobtrusively at it. 'How nice of you to have spared time and come . . .'

'Nanda, Nanda,' Ila interrupted with a cry and caught Nanda Kaul's hand and clung to it. 'Spared you time? My dear, you can't imagine, you have no idea what it has meant to me to have you here at Carignano, to come and see you today. Why, it's been a little bit of the past come alive. As if the past still existed here and I could simply come and visit it and have a cup of tea with it when I was tired of the present!'

Nanda Kaul's fine lips made a faint grimace at this that Ila Das noticed but could not interpret. So she wrung her admired friend's hands, crunching two large rings together with a grinding sound as she did so, and went on 'And to meet your great-grandchild – my, that was a pleasure!' Screwing up her little button eyes, she added 'Funny little thing, isn't she? I couldn't make her out – she's as secretive as a little wild bird, or an insect that hides, isn't she?'

'A little shy,' Nanda Kaul murmured. 'But she's been ill – with typhoid – and now it is her mother who is ill.'

'Dear, dear, I *am* sorry, I *am* sorry.' One more gigantic sigh exploded from Ila Das. 'Isn't the world full of troubles wherever you look? In my village, out of my village – it's the same everywhere.' Dropping Nanda Kaul's hand, she fixed her cloth bag firmly to her shoulder, gave her umbrella a decisive little swing and said 'Well, we must do the best we can about it. That's it, isn't it? We must simply shoulder our responsibilities and do what we can. Well,

Nanda. Well, my dear,' and raising herself on tiptoe, she pecked Nanda Kaul's cheek swiftly, then went down the hill, crying 'Thank you, thank you, my dear, so much. Bye-bye, bye-bye,' she went on calling, like a late cuckoo, all the way down to the chestnut trees on the Mall.

Nanda Kaul leant with both hands on the gate, watching her clumsy, floundering descent. She stood there with a rigidity in her posture, an intensity, almost quivering with the horrors of that afternoon as she watched them retreat. Yes, Ila Das brought horror with her and horror it was that hovered about her as she went off, as jerky and crazy as an old puppet, with her ancient umbrella and tattered bag. There had never been anyone more doomed, more menaced than she, thought Nanda Kaul, and how she survived at all – just by the barest skin of her teeth, by the weakest thread – was beyond her understanding. Her rackety existence looked so precarious, she felt that one stone thrown, one stick tipped would be enough to end it.

So she leaned upon the gate and watched over her with a kind of fierceness. She, well and strong and upright, she ought to protect her. She ought to fight some of her battles. She looked slowly up and down the length of the Mall to see if the way were safe for Ila Das, and if one derisive urchin had appeared then, or if one alarming *langur* had let itself down from the trees and made for Ila Das then, Nanda Kaul would have swooped to attack and demolish him. She would have attacked any mocking urchin, any vicious *langur*, if it had meant tearing through the dust, tearing her sari or even making a fool of herself.

But the road was deserted. Except for a friendly red-haired dog with a graceful plume for a tail that ran sniffing along the side of the road, there was not a soul on the Mall just then. Ila Das was plodding along, past the club, her figure growing more and more absurdly tiny and puppet-

133

like by the minute, till she reached the giant deodar by the red letter-box and then vanished.

Nanda Kaul relaxed and her hands released the gate which whined complainingly into place. She felt danger pass for the third time that afternoon. There had been the moment when Ila Das babbled maniacally about mixed doubles at the Vice-Chancellor's badminton party – that had passed. Then there had been the moment when she felt she must invite Ila Das to stay – and that had passed. Now this final danger was over, too – a mere cloud sailing over the hills, followed by its little chill shadow, indigo on azure.

Raising her head, holding her hands behind her back, Nanda Kaul began to pace up and down in the garden. She wished Raka would appear, and knew she would not. But a day lily was in bloom and Nanda Kaul went slowly over to congratulate it on its well-formed, clear yellow flower that would be shrivelled by tomorrow.

As she stood gazing at it, fine green wires gripped the yellow petals, dipping them earthwards, and very cautiously a praying mantis lifted itself onto the flower, abandoning its perfect camouflage to display the brilliant green of its body, face, legs and eyes on the waxy yellow petals. Then, becoming aware of Nanda Kaul's still, opaline presence, it lifted itself up on its hind legs, as if in self-defence, and raised its tiny hands together under its chin, turning its solemn head from side to side as it studied her with exactly the same serene curiosity that marked her face.

She put out her ringed hand and gave the lily a little shake so that the creature tumbled off into the leaves. There it would be safe from the birds.

Chapter 11

Ila Das did not take the Garkhal road that led down the hillside to her village, no. Buoyed up by Nanda Kaul's friendliness, by the tea, she gave her umbrella a cheerful swing and decided to visit the bazaar. Perhaps she would find something cheap there. If the price of corn meal had come down, she might buy half a kilo – corn meal *roti* was good, satisfying. Or potatoes – what would they cost now? she wondered. Well, if she couldn't afford to buy any, she could at least take a look and see what was available that she might purchase the day she got her salary. That *glad* day!

The thought of it made her lift her little feet and plod through the summer dust and get past all the staring groups of summer visitors who could not restrain their surprise and sometimes their laughter at the sight of her odd, jerky figure. Thinking of Nanda Kaul, how beautiful she still was, how gracefully she poured the tea, how sympathetically she listened, Ila Das barely noticed them.

Then a boy rolling along an old bicycle wheel for a hoop, gave an angry shout and shoved her aside, almost into the ditch outside the Pasteur Institute gate. But Ila Das only looked up at the great factory-like edifice and wondered, wished a job could be found for her there. Should she apply to the director? Should she confront him in his office? Ah, but what qualifications could she present, what particular job could she possibly apply for, or even covet? She grimaced at her audacity, biting her lips with her shining dentures. A jeep roared uphill in first gear, covering her with dust from top to toe.

She stood blinded and choked, and had to take off her spectacles and take out a handkerchief to wipe them before she could replace them crookedly on her nose and see anything. What she saw was a bunch of schoolgirls in bright indigo *salwar-kameez*, doubling up with laughter to see her blink and ruffle and shake like a little owl that had ventured out at the wrong time of day.

Ignoring them, Ila Das went on, rather less cheerfully. As she passed the Tibetan shawl sellers who had spread out their bright, cheap woollen ware on the street, she looked at their babies and puppies gambolling together in the middle of the road with a fine carelessness that she envied. There was a zest about them, a warmth of life's fires burning brightly in their shabby, grubby bodies, fires that had died out in her long ago, leaving this heap of ashes, this pain.

Down the twisting bazaar lane she hopped and hobbled, but it was so unfortunate how people invariably knocked into her or shoved her aside, burst into guffaws or made jeering remarks, as though her feelings didn't matter to anyone. Did they think she didn't feel it? So she lifted her chin high, very high, and her eyes blinked behind the bi-focals uncontrollably, but she gripped her umbrella tightly and went on. No one noticed anything staunch or splendid about her trembling chin, her wobbling top-knot or her hurried walk.

No one noticed except the grainseller at whose open shop she stopped because it was less crowded than the plastic buckets shop, the shoemaker's shop, the readymade garments and the hardware shop.

The grainseller – an elderly, whiskered man in a singlet and very clean, white cotton pyjamas – sat idly sifting pulses through his fingers, occasionally twisting his moustaches as he took in the bustling scene. He looked benevolently at Ila Das bending over the open sacks. He knew Ila Das. Whenever she got her salary, she came to his shop for what were supposed to be her month's provisions, only the shopkeeper knew they couldn't possibly last more than a fortnight – not even for such a child-sized and time-shrivelled creature. He would always throw in a free handful of red chillies or some cloves of garlic which was generous of him for they were expensive – only, unfortunately, Ila Das ate neither. She always thanked him effusively, however, and made him feel kindly towards her. His own daughter was club-footed – why should he laugh at this poor creature's deformities?

As if to flaunt her singular deformity, Ila Das brayed aloud 'The corn meal here – has the price come down at last?'

He leant across and scooped some up in a metal scoop that he held out for her to examine. 'Four rupees a kilo only,' he said.

Ila Das's spectacles slipped off her nose in horror. She quickly picked them up and collected herself, and the cool way in which she shook her head and moved on to the bins full of potatoes and onions would not have done discredit to her elegant mother.

But what *could* she buy here for her dinner? she wondered, again clutching her lower lip with those gleaming dentures. She thought of the few coins at the bottom of the cloth bag and shifted it on her shoulder and decided not to spend them. They had to last her quite a while. Perhaps, when she went home, she would find something on the kitchen shelf or in the dark corner where she hadn't looked properly. Bursting into a casual little hum, she turned around and said '*Achha*, I'll come again' to the shopkeeper, in a gay and careless way, and made to go.

He said suddenly, 'Are you going home now, Memsahib?'

'Yes,' she said, surprised, stopping to look at him.

'You shouldn't go so late,' he said, and his face was

137

troubled behind the profusion of whiskers. 'It is not good for a memsahib to walk alone in the dark.'

'Why?' she laughed, her teeth gleaming, her voice raw because she was touched at his concern. 'I am always alone. I am never afraid.'

He did not say anything more, only shook his head and kept an eye on her as she made her way back through the bazaar with her empty bag, skirting the *pai* dogs that barked and tumbled in a muddy knot, past the crowds outside the sweetmeat shop where great pans of milk steamed and flies rose and settled in clouds on pyramids of pink and yellow and green sweets and the discarded papers and leaf-cups in the open drain.

He thought of Preet Singh who lived in the same village as Ila Das and had passed the time of morning with him earlier today and spoken of Ila Das, how she was trying to stop him marrying off his daughter to a rich landowner who had made a good offer for her. Preet Singh had spat and cursed Ila Das, using coarse, obscene words that made the grainseller fall silent in disapproval. He himself knew a Memsahib when he saw one. Such obscenity upset him as a badly cooked meal might. Watching Ila Das clumsily pick her way through a marble game in the road, he frowned with uneasiness. It was growing dark.

Made conscious of the dark by the grainseller, Ila Das hurried out of the bazaar and past the shops on the Mall in a kind of panic that made her chin jerk up and down and her cheeks flop in and out. It had been a mistake not to go home immediately, to waste time at the bazaar. What a fool to go shopping when she had no money! Vexed with herself, she shook her head violently. The top-knot tumbled down her neck.

Summer visitors at the Alasia Hotel, looking down from the terrace where they sat with their drinks, thought her the crazy woman, walking jerkily and talking to herself, that

138

every holiday resort seems to have at least one of, for their pity or amusement. They turned to each other and smiled, dipped their heads and drank.

Once under the chestnut trees of the Lower Mall, Ila Das tried to tease herself out of her panic. Why was she afraid? Of whom? She was not in debt to anyone in the bazaar. No, Ila Das would never take a loan, never. Ooh, what would her father have thought if she had? She gave a little spurting giggle at the thought of her father, in his fawn waistcoat with the gold watch–chain cascading out of a pocket, knowing his daughter, groomed by a long line of governesses and ayahs, to be in debt to some hairy, half-dressed shopkeeper.

But here she stopped herself. Why did she think of that kindly concerned man in the grainshop as hairy, half-dressed? Now when would she ever get over that pompous education of hers, leave it all behind and learn to deal with the world, now her world, as it was?

Well, she was trying. Just stopping herself from stepping into a cowpat, Ila Das hurried on through the cold, fretted shade of the chestnut trees, only half-hearing the hoots of laughter from the children on the hillside who had seen her skip, goat-like, over the cowpat. She knew they would have loved to see her fall into it. Ooh dear, she couldn't tell who she feared more – jeering urchins or the marauding *langurs* that sometimes waylaid her and terrified her by baring their teeth and chattering insults at her. The way was full of hazards, full of hazards. The grainseller was right. She trembled.

She came to the fork and hurriedly, without stopping, took the steeply plunging footpath that would take her down, down the hillside to her village.

Chapter 12

Leaving behind the last of the shabby, rundown houses and dried up, untended gardens of the town, Ila Das began to hop, skip and slide down the footpath to her village, already lost in the evening shadow of the mountains. She hoped to be home before night.

There were only a few more farmhouses on the way — solid, square houses built of Kasauli fieldstone, with pumpkins and corn drying on their roofs, goats tied to the doorposts, women noisily dipping brass pots into barrels of water. Dogs barked to see her go. Some of the women called in jeering but not unfriendly voices, as to a funny child. She waved her umbrella at them — she had visited them just that morning to explain the benefits of vaccination to them — and then went down, down the steep path between great rocks and black, windwhipped pine trees.

The last of the light had left the valley. It was already a deep violet and only the Kasauli ridge, where Carignano stood invisibly, was still bright with sunlight, russet and auburn, copper and brass. An eagle took off from the peak of Monkey Point, lit up like a torch in the sky, and dropped slowly down into the valley, lower and lower, till it was no more than a sere leaf, a scrap of burnt paper, drifting on currents of air, silently.

Although it had been hot all day, now there was a chill like a white mist beginning to creep out of the shadows of the great jagged rocks and filter through the pine trees and set Ila Das, in her frayed, worn laces and silks, shivering. The day gone, the light gone, the warmth of life gone, it was like wandering lost in a Chinese landscape – an austere pen and ink scroll, of rocks and pines and mountain peaks, all muted by mist, by darkness.

So sad, so *triste*, thought Ila Das, her teeth chattering as she clutched her umbrella to her chest and stumbled over pebbles and rocks. To be alone, to be old, to have to walk this long, sad distance down this desolate hillside, it was more than she could bear. Oh, she could bear it just now, she said, clenching her lower lip with her teeth, but how much longer? how much longer?

The last of the rooks had left the sky, had stopped circling and searching above the pines, and settled for the night. There was no sign of life, no sound. Only little Ila Das scuttling through the Chinese landscape, a little frightened spider in this vast, chilly web. How she hurried, hurried to escape it. How she wished she had asked – had forced herself to ask – Nanda Kaul to give her a room at Carignano, allow her to stay with her, or at least begged the kind grainseller for half a kilo of corn meal for her dinner. But, because of her absurd pride in being her father's daughter, her ridiculous failure ever to forget it, she had not asked, had not begged, and so she was stumbling through the rocks alone, climbing over the charred, twisted tree-trunks that lay across the path, to the crumbling hut of mud and thatch near the earthen heap of the hamlet, to search on the empty shelf for a scrap of food and to lie awake through the night on a flea-ridden string cot.

But that was all she had. That was what she was scurrying towards. Lord, it was late. Mist – now, in summer? And so cold? She held the umbrella against her thin chest and edged past a particularly large and murderous agave, then climbed down a slippery pile of pebbles spattered with goat droppings.

Now at last she came to the final fold of the hill. Once around it, she would be home. Almost running, almost throwing herself at that last big rock in her way, Ila Das could see it – the hamlet – just below her. There was the farmhouse, long and low and built of stone, red-roofed, with all the tumbling outhouses about it, thatch-roofed, with saffron ears of corn drying in bunches from their eaves. There it was – the hamlet – perched above a long skirt of terraced fields in which the ripe, ready wheat stood blond and brittle and potato vines spread themselves over the loamy earth. There was the big tank of rainwater in which frogs plopped and rkk-rkk-rkked aloud, under the pomegranate trees with their little tight scarlet pom-poms of bloom. There were the cows coming down the upper path, their bells lugubriously tolling, their sweet smell of warm, chewed straw carrying over to her. At their heels came barking and lolloping the handsome red dog with the plumed tail that Nanda Kaul had seen snuffing along the Upper Mall. No lamps had been lit yet – the people were poor and frugal – but, in a little while, the first pinprick would start into the dark, then three or four. Ila Das, too, would light her lamp in which there was still a little kerosene.

At the thought of the lamp flowering into light in her dark hut, at the thought of the cows comfortably mooing and chewing in the lean-to next to her, she stopped under the looming rock, caught her breath and narrowed her little eyes with pleasure, with relief.

Just then a black shape detached itself from the jagged pile of the rock, that last rock between her and the hamlet, and sprang soundlessly at her. She staggered under its weight with a gasp that ripped through her chest. It had her by the throat. She struggled, choking, trying to stretch and stretch and stretch that gasp till it became a shout, a shout that the villagers would hear, the red dog would hear, a shout for help. But the fingers tightened. Now she tore her mouth open for breath, now she opened her eyes till they boggled, and popped, and stood out of her head as she saw, in the cold shadow, that it was Preet Singh, his lips lifted back from his teeth, his eyes blazing down at her in rage, in a passion of rage. She lifted her hands to dislodge his from her throat and she did dislodge them. They fell away, but only to tear at the cotton scarf that hung about his neck, only to wrap that about her throat, tighter, tighter, tighter, so that the last gasp rattled inside her, choked and rattled and was still. Her eyes still swivelled in their sockets, two alarmed marbles of black and white, and quickly he left the ends of the scarf, tore at her clothes, tore them off her, in long, screeching rips, till he came to her, to the dry, shrivelled, starved stick inside the wrappings, and raped her, pinned her down into the dust and the goat droppings, and raped her. Crushed back, crushed down into the earth, she lay raped, broken, still and finished. Now it was dark.

Chapter 13

When the sharp, long sliver of the telephone's call cut through the dusk, Nanda Kaul stopped, clapping her hands together in anger. The telephone again – no! But it couldn't be Ila Das. Ila Das had only left an hour or so ago, it could not be her again. Perhaps it was a wrong number. She would not go in. It was still so lovely here – the blue shadows of night spilling across the garden like cool water, the crickets putting out their song one by one, the lights beginning to flower on the distant hilltops, hazily. Let it ring. Ring, ring, ring.

Then Ram Lal came out of the kitchen, strode across the yard in steps the shadows made even longer, till he was in the house and had silenced, decapitated the telephone.

143

She relaxed. She walked on, disturbing a silver-dusted moth on a fuchsia that swung free and fluttered away. Let Ram Lal answer the phone, let others answer such demands, such intrusions. She wanted only to be alone in the garden in the dark.

But Ram Lal came out onto the veranda and replaced the shrill peremptoriness of the 'phone by his deep voice calling 'Memsahib, 'phone for you.'

She gave her ringed fingers a little twist of irritation. Could she not be left alone? After this dreadful, tangled afternoon with Ila Das screaming and braying into her ear by the hour, could she not be given a quiet hour in which to recover, to take in the pine-tinged evening air and recover?

She swept up the flagstones of the path like an aroused snake, mounted the veranda steps and went up to the table where the telephone lay, in two divided halves, black, beside the open window from which the sky looked in, pale and muted. Sitting down on the little stool, she picked up the receiver and said 'Yes?'

'This is P. K. Shukla, madam, police officer in charge, Garkhal *thana*,' said a brisk, quick voice that brushed aside her sighs, her innuendoes. 'You know Miss Ila Das, welfare officer of the Garkhal division?'

'Yes,' frowned Nanda Kaul, lifting one hand to her temple. 'Yes?'

'Your name and telephone number were found on a piece of paper in her bag. Kindly come to the police station at the earliest to identify her body.'

Nanda Kaul's head twisted back, back. She lowered her hand from her temple to her throat and clutched it. 'Ila?' she murmured. 'Ila Das?'

'Yes, madam,' the sure voice repeated, slightly impatient of her histrionics. 'Her body was found on the path to the village Timarpur. She was found by the villagers. She has been strangled. The doctor is here. He claims she has been

144

raped. She is dead. Kindly come to the police station at the earliest to identify . . .'

But Nanda Kaul had ceased to listen. She had dropped the telephone. With her head still thrown back, far back, she gasped: No, no, it is a lie! No, it cannot be. It was a lie – Ila was not raped, not dead. It was all a lie, all. She had lied to Raka, lied about everything. Her father had never been to Tibet – he had bought the little Buddha from a travelling pedlar. They had not had bears and leopards in their home, nothing but overfed dogs and bad-tempered parrots. Nor had her husband loved and cherished her and kept her like a queen – he had only done enough to keep her quiet while he carried on a lifelong affair with Miss David, the mathematics mistress, whom he had not married because she was a Christian but whom he had loved, all his life loved. And her children – the children were all alien to her nature. She neither understood nor loved them. She did not live here alone by choice – she lived here alone because that was what she was forced to do, reduced to doing. All those graces and glories with which she had tried to captivate Raka were only a fabrication: they helped her to sleep at night, they were tranquillizers, pills. She had lied to Raka. And Ila had lied, too. Ila, too, had lied, had tried. No, she wanted to tell the man on the phone, No, she wanted to cry, but could not make a sound. Instead, it choked and swelled inside her throat. She twisted her head, then hung it down, down, let it hang.

There was a scratching at the window that turned to a tapping, then a drumming. 'Nani, Nani,' whispered Raka, shivering and crouching in the lily bed, peeping over the sill. 'Look, Nani, I have set the forest on fire. Look, Nani – look – the forest is on fire.' Tapping, then drumming, she raised her voice, then raised her head to look in and saw Nanda Kaul on the stool with her head hanging, the black telephone hanging, the long wire dangling.

Down in the ravine, the flames spat and crackled around the dry wood and through the dry grass, and black smoke spiralled up over the mountain.

BY ANITA DESAI
ALSO AVAILABLE IN VINTAGE

☐ **Baumgartner's Bombay**	0099428520	£6.99
☐ **Clear Light of Day**	0099276186	£6.99
☐ **Diamond Dust**	0099289644	£6.99
☐ **Fasting, Feasting**	0099289636	£6.99
☐ **Games at Twilight**	0099428539	£6.99
☐ **In Custody**	0099428490	£6.99
☐ **Journey to Ithaca**	0099428474	£6.99

FREE POST AND PACKING
Overseas customers allow £2.00 per paperback

BY PHONE: 01624 677237

BY POST: Random House Books
C/o Bookpost, PO Box 29, Douglas
Isle of Man, IM99 1BQ

BY FAX: 01624 670923

BY EMAIL: bookshop@enterprise.net

Cheques (payable to Bookpost) and credit cards accepted

Prices and availability subject to change without notice.
Allow 28 days for delivery.
When placing your order, please mention if you do not wish to receive
any additional information.

www.randomhouse.co.uk/vintage